The Happy Hollisters and the Old Clipper Ship

BY JERRY WEST

Illustrated by Helen S. Hamilton

GARDEN CITY, N.Y.

Doubleday & Company, Inc.

Contents

CHAPTER 1

ACTION! CAMERA!

CRACK! BOOM!

A deafening thunderclap shook the house and rattled the windows in the attic where the five Hollister children were playing.

"Crickets, that lightning was close!" Pete Hollister exclaimed. The twelve-year-old boy blinked his blue eyes, then added, "Let's go on with the show."

Pete was standing behind an upended steamer trunk on which rested a home movie camera. Two big floodlights brightened the scene.

"Tell us when to start again," Pam said cheerily.

The golden-haired girl, who was ten, knelt on one knee beside an orange crate. On top of it was four-year-old Sue, the dark-haired baby of the family. She giggled at two other children, who stood off to one side.

They were Ricky, seven, and Holly, six. Ricky's red hair was mussed and his freckled face beamed with excitement. "Come on, Pete," he said eagerly, "let 'er roll!"

Holly fidgeted, twirling her brown pigtails as she waited for cameraman Pete's orders.

"All right!" the older boy said. "Don't forget,

5

Pam. You're supposed to be in a lifeboat looking up at the deck of the old clipper ship. Sue, you're about to be washed away by a big wave, and Holly and Ricky will save you. Are you ready?"

The four other children nodded and Pete said, "Here we go!"

Pam immediately looked as worried as she could. "Please save my baby, please save her!" she cried, clasping her hands dramatically.

"We will!" Ricky assured her as he and Holly advanced toward the orange crate.

Reeling from side to side as if they were on the deck of an old clipper ship caught in a bad storm, Ricky and Holly made a cradle seat with their hands, scooping up their little sister.

"We'll carry her to the other lifeboat," Holly said. At this, Sue burst out giggling and Pete, crying "Cut!" stopped the camera.

As Sue hopped to the floor, Pete said, "You can't laugh in this scene. You're supposed to be frightened, Sue."

"But it's so funny," the little girl said, her eyes twinkling.

"That's not the way actresses perform," Pam told her. "Now we'll have to do it all over again."

"And I don't have too much film left," Pete said.

As the rain beat down hard on the attic roof, the Hollister children prepared to re-enact the scene. Playing movies was a rainy-day game which

6

pleased all of them. Recently they had read in the newspaper that Lisa Sarno and Gregory Grant, famous film stars, were about to act in a movie called *The Old Clipper Ship*. Now Pam was playing the part of Lisa and Ricky was supposed to be Gregory.

The children had learned about United States clipper ships which used to carry on trade with China. They set out from the New England coast for the long, dangerous voyages to the Far East. So Pam had written a little story about the wreck of such a ship and Pete was acting as both cameraman and director.

As lightning flashed again and thunder boomed in the distance, Pete made ready for another shot. "Action!" he called out.

This time the scene went well. Sue wrinkled up her face to look as if she were crying, as Ricky and Holly carried her off to safety.

"Ready for the next scene!" Pete ordered.

"What's this to be?" Ricky asked, turning to Pam. His older sister had a pad of notes in her hand.

"I'll look at the script," she said. "Oh yes, this is where Sue climbs down a rope hanging from the side of the ship and lands in the lifeboat."

Quickly pulling a stepladder from the corner of the attic, Ricky placed it beneath a rafter. Then, holding a piece of rope, he climbed up and tied it securely over the rafter. In the meantime Pam

"Climb down slowly," Pam called.

set up one side of a cardboard rowboat—the side facing the camera.

"Do you think Sue can climb down the rope?" Pete asked, running a hand through his blond crewcut.

"Sure I can," the little girl piped up.

"All right," Pete agreed, and added, "Ricky, you'd better stand by to catch her if she falls."

When everything was ready for the scene, Sue climbed the ladder and grabbed hold of the rope. Then Ricky pulled the ladder away.

"Climb down slowly!" Pam called out as Pete started his "take."

Sue was halfway down the rope when suddenly another loud clap of thunder rattled the windows. The noise startled the little girl. "Help! Help!" she cried. "I—I'm going to fall!"

Ricky dashed toward her. But in doing so he tripped over the side of the boat and landed flat on his face at the end of the rope. Sue fell *kerplunk* on top of her brother!

"Oof!" Ricky grunted, the breath knocked out of him for a moment.

Pete stopped the camera and he and Pam rushed over to pick up Sue. "Are you hurt?" he asked.

"No," she said, laughing, "but I'm afraid I hurt Lifeboat Ricky."

The red-haired boy took a deep breath. "Yikes!

I don't want to play lifeboat again," he said ruefully.

"Do we have to shoot that scene over?" Holly asked.

"No," Pete replied. "That was a good shot!"

The noise of the wind and rain grew louder as the summer storm mounted in fury. Suddenly there was an ear-splitting crack. The thunder and lightning seemed to come together. The floodlights went out. This was followed by a ripping sound from outside—a noise that sounded like crashing metal.

"Oh dear!" Pam called out. "The lightning has struck something!"

"I think the sound came from the street," Pete put in. "Come on, let's go and see."

At this moment the lights went on again. But the experience had shaken them. They decided to stop their game. Pete opened the attic door and they all tramped down to the second floor.

The five Hollister children and their parents lived in a large, rambling house in the friendly town of Shoreham on Pine Lake. Down in the business section Mr. Hollister, a tall, rugged, outdoor man, had a combination hardware, sports, and toy shop. He called it *The Trading Post*. He and Mrs. Hollister, slender and pretty, were always ready to share in their youngsters' adventures.

As the children reached the first floor, Zip,

their beautiful collie dog, bounded out of the kitchen to meet them. Thunderstorms made him nervous, so Pam, in her kindly way, patted him comfortingly.

"Don't worry, Zip, it'll soon be over," she said, then followed the others to the front porch.

Mrs. Hollister, wearing a raincoat and hat, was already out there, peering across the wide lawn through the teeming sheet of rain. There was no more thunder or lightning. "What a terrible crash!" she said as the others crowded around her in the darkness of the storm.

"We thought it hit something nearby," Ricky stated. "Let's find out." He and the other children dashed back inside to put on raincoats and sou'westers. Pete grabbed a flashlight.

"Do any of you see where it might have struck?" Mrs. Hollister asked when they returned.

"I think I see a car," Pete answered, straining his eyes and flashing his light.

"Look!" Pam suddenly shouted. "There *is* a car, right in front of our house. And a tree limb has fallen on it!"

Just then the Hollisters heard a voice cry out, "Help! Help! Get me out!"

"Somebody's trapped inside!" Pete cried. "Come on!"

Without a moment's hesitation, Mrs. Hollister and the children ran down the porch steps and across the lawn toward the wrecked automobile.

CHAPTER 2

UP A TREE

As THE Hollisters dashed toward the car, the cries for help from inside it started once more. Reaching the two-door sedan at the curb, they found its hood nearly covered by a large limb which had cracked off from the tree alongside it. Slumped over the steering wheel was a young man, now semi-conscious.

"Oh, he's hurt!" Holly cried as they all peered anxiously through the closed window.

"We'll get him out," Pete said, and ran around to the driver's side. He turned the handle and tried to open the door, but it would not budge.

"The frame has sprung from the impact," Pete called out. "Try the one on your side, Pam!"

Both Pam and her mother endeavored to open the other door but this one was locked. The driver, meanwhile, continued to moan and turn his head from side to side.

"Oh dear, we *must* get him out!" Mrs. Hollister exclaimed.

"I know how we can do it!" Pete shouted, and dashed to the Hollisters' garage.

He returned a few moments later with a heavy crowbar. Pressing the point of the tool along the side of the door on the driver's side, Pete pushed hard.

CRUNCH! The door creaked open, and as it did, the stranger inside began slipping toward the street. But Pete quickly grasped him by the shoulders.

"Help me get him to the house," he said.

Pam, meanwhile, had gone for a blanket. Now the man was laid on the improvised stretcher and carried to the house.

"He has a bad gash on his forehead!" Pam exclaimed, opening the door.

By this time the pelting rain had revived the fellow somewhat. His eyes, previously almost closed, now opened wider, but he seemed too dazed to speak. They took him into the living room and laid him on a sofa. Holly propped a pillow under his head.

"Lie still," Mrs. Hollister said kindly.

"I'll bring the first-aid kit, Mother," Pam offered, and hurried upstairs to the medicine cabinet.

Pete loosened the man's collar and Ricky removed his shoes. Holly tucked the blanket around him.

"I—I feel all right now," the man protested, trying to rise from the sofa.

"Please, don't try to get up yet," Mrs. Hollister said as Pam brought the first-aid kit. The two deftly cleaned the cut and wrapped a bandage about the man's head.

"Thank you, thank you all so much," he said, lying back on the sofa again. "My name is Tom King."

"And we're the Happy Hollisters." Sue spoke up eagerly. "At least that's what people call us."

The visitor smiled. Now that the first shock of the excitement had worn off and it appeared certain that Tom King had not suffered serious injury, the children took a closer look at him. He was a slender, handsome man, very suntanned, with jet-black hair. Although dressed in slacks, a sport shirt, and a bright-colored tie like many men in Shoreham, he did not look exactly like any of them.

"Maybe he's from outer space," Ricky whispered to his brother.

But the young man heard it, and smiled for the second time, showing fine even, white teeth.

"No, I'm not from Mars——" He grinned weakly. "I'm part Polynesian—from the Territory of Hawaii."

"How very interesting!" Mrs. Hollister remarked. "It's a shame you've had an accident, especially when you are so far away from home."

"So that's what happened to me," the man said. "My memory seems to be a bit blank right now."

As Tom King rested, the children quickly told

14

They carried the stranger on the improvised cot.

him about the crash they had heard while in the attic.

"You were good to get me out of the car," the young man said gratefully. "The last I remember is driving down this street, then a terrific crash and being thrown against the steering wheel. Lucky for me the branch didn't land on the roof and crash through."

By now the storm was over and daylight had returned. "Let's go look at the car," Ricky proposed, and ran outside, but no one followed.

Peering inside, the boy noticed a suitcase on the floor by the back seat. Ricky picked up the bag and carried it into the house.

"I thought you might need this," he said to Tom King.

"Thank you, Ricky, but I'll be going soon."

"You can't," the boy told him. "Your car won't move."

"And you had a terrible bang." Sue spoke up. "You ought to put on your 'jamas and go to bed."

This made Tom King chuckle. "I can't impose upon you all much longer," he said.

"You must stay with us until you feel stronger," Mrs. Hollister said. "Pam, will you make some tea for our guest?"

"Thank you very much," Tom King said. "That will be fine. It may chase away my headache."

While the tea was being prepared, Pete went to the telephone to report that the tree limb lay across the road. He dialed the police department.

"May I speak to Officer Cal?" he asked.

As the boy waited, he recalled the first time the Hollisters had met the kind young policeman. The family had just moved to Shoreham, and one of their furniture vans had been stolen. Officer Cal helped them find it, and the children in turn had assisted him in rounding up the thief.

"Hello, Cal," Pete said, and told what had happened.

It seemed to the boy as if he had hardly hung up when Cal and another officer were on the scene in a police car. The children rushed out to see them.

"This is a job for both the wrecking crew and the tree department," Cal remarked, glancing first at the car and then to the top of the tree from which the branch had been torn by the lightning.

The young, rosy-cheeked policeman thanked the children for calling up and added, "I'll give a complete report of this to headquarters right away."

Getting back into his car, he picked up the radio telephone and asked for a crew from the town's tree department to come to the Hollisters' home immediately. He hung up and stepped from the car.

"I'll go see this Mr. King now," he said, and led the way into the house. Pete introduced the two men.

"Perhaps you'd better go to the hospital, Mr. King," Cal suggested, "to be sure no bones are broken."

But the injured man assured him that, aside from the cut on his forehead and a feeling of shakiness, he was all right.

"We'll see that he's well taken care of," Mrs. Hollister said.

"I'm sure you will," Cal replied, smiling. Then he added, "The Hollisters seem to make everybody happy, even if the sky falls in on them."

"As it almost did on me," the Hawaiian remarked, winking at Sue. This made everybody laugh.

Then the policeman continued, "We'll have your car towed to a garage, Mr. King, and if you like, they'll repair the hood for you."

"Fine. I'd appreciate that," the man replied.

"And let us know how you are tomorrow," the officer said.

After Cal had left, Mrs. Hollister noticed that Tom King was becoming drowsy, and motioned the children to leave the room. They tiptoed out of the house and went to the curb to wait for the garage tow truck.

Pete tried to close the car door which he had pried open. It would not shut and the boy was a little worried.

"The repairmen will take care of it, Pete," Pam said consolingly.

Ricky and Holly, meanwhile, had taken off their shoes and socks and were splashing their feet in the water running along the curb when two trucks—a black-and-white wrecking car from Tony's Garage and the tree department's big vehicle with all kinds of tree equipment—pulled up.

By now many neighborhood children had begun to gather. Among them were Jeff and Ann Hunter, special friends of Ricky and Pam. Jeff was eight and had dark straight hair and blue eyes. Ann was ten. She had gray eyes and dark curly hair that hung in ringlets. The damp weather made them spring up and down as she turned her head.

As the three treemen lifted the limb from the car with a crane, the Hollisters' friends plied them with questions.

"Did you see that big branch fall?"

"I'll bet it was a terrible crash!"

"Was anybody hurt?"

The Hollisters answered all the questions.

"And you say Tom King is from somewhere in the Hawaiian Islands?" Ann asked. "Is he going to live here now?"

"We don't know," Pam answered.

Before the girls could discuss this further, the man from the garage called out, "All right. Stand back!"

His workmen now attached a chain to the front of Tom King's car and it was hoisted into the air. The motor of the truck started up, and soon the disabled car was being hauled away down the street.

As the treemen prepared to continue their work, Pam said, "Oh, I do hope the beautiful elm isn't ruined entirely."

"No, it'll be all right," said the foreman reassuringly. He told the children his name was Nick.

"What do you have to do now?" Pete asked him.

"Cut the limb up with our power saw."

While the other men were doing this, Nick looked up at the towering elm and said, "I see that another branch has been splintered, so we'll have to cut it off near the trunk."

The foreman placed two signs in the street which read: *Drive slowly. Men working.*

Then he went to the back of the truck and pulled out a large coil of rope. Deftly swinging one end of it, he hurled the rope high into the air. It fell over one of the branches and down the other side. As soon as the other men had finished their job, they came to help him.

The children looked on in amazement as they prepared for their work. How nimble the men were! One fastened the rope around his waist and, carrying his saw, hoisted himself high into the tree.

"Look out below, you kids!" he cried. "I'm going to start cutting this limb."

Everyone moved back quickly to a safe distance while the tree surgeon's saw flashed back and forth.

"Yikes, he's strong!" Ricky said, observing the tireless motion of the man's muscular arm. "That's what I want to be when I grow up—a tree surgeon."

The man in the tree stopped his sawing and looked down. "Okay, Nick!" he shouted. "She's ready to fall!"

The foreman ordered all the children to stand back even farther until they were in a big circle some yards away from the tree. Then he called to Pete:

"Would you like to help us by stopping traffic down the street while we drop this limb?"

"Oh yes."

Pete hurried off to the nearby corner. When two cars came along, he raised his arm and let out a shrill whistle. The drivers halted and the boy explained.

Ricky, watching his brother, wished to help too. He decided that he would stop the traffic coming from the other direction. Without noticing that the tree surgeon was beginning to saw again, Ricky made a dash under the tree. Just then the big limb went crack!

"There she goes!" the man shouted. At the same instant Nick called in alarm, "Get out of there, boy!"

Crash! The big limb went crashing down, only inches behind Ricky!

"Oh!" Pam cried, weak from fright.

"I—I only wanted to stop the cars coming the other way," Ricky explained sheepishly.

"Okay, you do that!" Nick said, mopping his brow with a handkerchief. "Only stay away from this tree!"

Ricky stopped one car as it approached. Then, with all the traffic held back, the treeman sawed off the remainder of the broken limb. With the agility of a monkey, he let himself down the rope to the street again. Within a few minutes the treemen had lifted the big limb onto the side of the road, where they proceeded to cut it up. Pete and Ricky waved the traffic to come through.

"Thanks for helping us," Nick said, giving Ricky a rueful grin. "Only next time——"

"I won't," Ricky broke in earnestly. "Not ever again."

It did not take the men long to pile up the logs and put their equipment back onto the truck. Nick and his crew jumped into the cab and, waving to the children, pulled away.

At that moment Holly shouted, "Here comes Dad!"

A station wagon came down the street and turned into the Hollisters' driveway. The driver smiled broadly as the five children raced over and he brought the car to a halt.

"Mother telephoned me about the accident," he said, getting out. "I hear we have a guest from the Territory of Hawaii."

"Yes," Sue piped up. "Come and meet him."

They found Tom King sitting up on the sofa.

"Tom King has agreed to stay awhile," Mrs. Hollister said, smiling.

"I surely appreciate your hospitality," the man said. "By the way, would one of you children please get my brief case from the car?"

"But your car's gone!" Ricky told him.

"It's probably at the garage now," Pete put in.

Tom King thought for a moment. "Well, I guess the case will be safe enough at the garage," he said finally. "I'll pick it up in the morning."

As the children listened intently, he told the Hollisters that he had been in the United States only a few weeks. "I bought my car on the Coast," he said. "I've been driving across the country asking questions of several people on the way."

"Questions?" Holly put in. "Are you a question man like they have on TV?"

This made Tom King grin. "No, but I do wish I knew the answer to a certain mystery!"

CHAPTER 3

A CURIOUS STRANGER

"You have a mystery to solve, Mr. King?" Holly cried. "Oh goody! We love to solve mysteries!"

"Then maybe you can help me," Tom King said. "And how about just calling me Tom?"

"What's your mystery about?" Pam asked eagerly.

"An inheritance," the visitor replied. "The story begins with my grandparents in Hawaii many years ago."

"They were Polynesians?" Pete inquired.

"Just my grandmother," Tom answered.

As the Hollister children listened wide-eyed, he told them that his grandfather, named Isaac Swanton, had been an American seaman from Boston. He had come to Honolulu on a clipper ship. "There he met and fell in love with my grandmother. She was a pure Polynesian."

"How romantic!" Pam sighed dreamily.

Tom said Isaac Swanton had married his sweetheart, named Kalua, aboard the clipper ship. The captain had performed the ceremony.

"And they lived happily ever after like Cinderella?" Holly burst out.

24

"They did," Tom replied, "and had several children. My mother was the youngest."

The young man went on to say that his grandparents had died before he was born so he never knew them. He himself was an only child and had been left an orphan when very young.

"I was brought up by one of my aunts," Tom added. He smiled. "None of the Hawaiian branch of the family had much money and I had to borrow some to go through college. So you can understand how an inheritance would be very helpful."

"Tell us more about it," Ricky begged as Tom paused.

"The inheritance is to come from a cousin William of mine who died last year. His family remained in the United States," Tom explained. "William's father was a brother to my grandfather, Isaac Swanton."

"Did you ever meet your cousin?" Pete asked.

"No. Our branch of the family in Honolulu was never in touch with any of the Swantons here. But one day we saw a Boston newspaper with an account of my cousin's death and the fact that the executors of his estate were looking for relatives of his.

"My cousin William had become a millionaire. But he never married and left no will. I'm here to represent the Hawaiian group."

25

The children listened wide-eyed to his story.

Pete looked perplexed. "Why can't you just collect the money?"

Tom shifted his position on the sofa and gave a wry smile. "It's not so easy as that. We have to prove we're descendants of Isaac Swanton. The only record of my grandparents' marriage was contained in the logbook of the clipper ship. The log has long since disappeared and there is no other written proof that the event took place. And, of course, any witnesses to the ceremony have died."

"What was the name of the clipper ship?" Pam asked.

"That's another problem," Tom replied. "I don't know. Neither my grandparents nor my parents mentioned the ship's name in any of their records or letters which I possess. But I do have one good clue."

"What's that?" Ricky asked.

"Grandfather left three detailed sketches of his clipper ship. Unfortunately the artist didn't include the name on any of them."

"May I see them sometime?" Pete requested. "I think old clipper ships were wonderful."

"They're in my brief case," Tom said. "That's why I was anxious to get it. But no doubt they'll be safe in the garage overnight."

The Hawaiian then went on to explain that the people he had contacted in his trip across the country, trying to pick up some information, were several elderly, retired seamen.

"One of them referred me to a Mr. Sparr here in Shoreham," Tom said. "I was on my way to see him when the storm stopped me. He may be able to identify Grandfather's ship from the drawings."

Pam smiled. "Mr. Sparr is a friend of ours, Tom, and knows a lot about sailing."

"He lent us a compass when we went to Sea Gull Beach." Sue spoke up.

"We lost it, but found it again," Pete chuckled. "That was a swell mystery."

Mrs. Hollister excused herself, saying she would start supper. Once more Tom King insisted he should leave, but the Hollisters would not hear of this. Pam went with her mother to assist in the kitchen while the others continued to chat.

"Tell me something else about yourselves," the visitor suggested.

The Islander chuckled as he listened to the children's various exploits. By the time they had finished, the tempting aroma of broiling lamb chops wafted in from the kitchen.

"I feel better already," Tom grinned. He stood up from the couch. "My legs aren't so wobbly and my headache's almost gone."

When the Hollisters and their guest sat down at the table, they all bowed their heads. It was Holly's turn to say grace, and she murmured,

"Bless, oh Lord, this food to our use and make us mindful of the needs of others."

A delightful meal followed, during which the conversation turned again to clipper ships.

"There's an old saying," Tom remarked, "that clipper ships were only thirty feet wide but a mile high."

Sue put down her fork, her eyes wide. "Oh, they must have touched the sky!" she exclaimed.

Tom smiled at the little girl. "The ships weren't really that tall," he said. "They only looked that way because of the height of the mast."

He explained that the clipper ship era began in 1843 because of the demand for more rapid delivery of tea from China. Their use declined with the opening of the Suez Canal in 1869 after which it was no longer necessary to sail around the tip of Africa to reach China.

"But steamships were much faster, weren't they?" Ricky asked.

Much to everyone's surprise, Tom said not always; that speed records held by the clippers lasted for twenty-five years after steamboats became popular.

"Some of them could make four hundred miles in twenty-four hours," the Hawaiian told them.

"You know so much about clipper ships, maybe you can help us in the movie we're making," Pam suggested.

"I'd be delighted to," Tom replied.

After dinner the children cleared the table and tidied up the kitchen. Then Pete led the way to the attic.

"This looks like a real Hollywood studio set," Tom remarked admiringly as the floodlights were turned on.

Holly was so excited about showing the studio to their guest that she skipped gaily across the attic. In doing so she tripped over the electric wires which led to the floodlights. The cord was yanked hard by the girl's foot and the big lamp started to tilt.

"Grab them!" Pete called out.

But no one was near enough to do this and the lights crashed to the floor, shattering in pieces.

"Oh dear!" Holly cried in dismay. "Look what I've done."

"No movie shooting tonight," Pete said, surveying the damage dejectedly.

"Well"—Tom King spoke up—"I know something that usually helps in disappointments."

"What's that?" Ricky asked eagerly.

"Ice cream."

"It sure does," Sue chimed in. "Only we haven't any left in our freezer."

"Is there a store nearby where we can get some?" Tom asked.

Sue nodded her head vigorously. "Real close."

30

"Then let's go," said the young man. "I feel strong enough to walk to the store. We'll order your favorite flavors."

"Oh yummy!" Holly giggled.

The Hollisters cascaded down the two flights of stairs, with Ricky sliding on the last few feet of banister as a short cut. A few moments later they were outside, walking toward the ice cream store. Ricky and Holly had fun jumping over puddles which lay here and there on the sidewalks.

Suddenly the children spied a boy riding a bicycle toward them. "Oh, here comes Joey Brill," Pam said.

"From your tone of voice, I guess you don't like him," Tom King remarked.

The Hollisters quickly explained that Joey, who was Pete's age but larger, had made trouble for the Hollisters ever since they had moved to Shoreham.

"He's an awful bully, but we try not to let him bother us," Holly said.

As Joey pedaled closer, he picked up speed. Suddenly, a few feet away, he veered over to the curb, where water still was standing.

Splash! His wheels threw up a spray which shot waist-high over the sidewalk. Everyone jumped aside, but Pam's white dress was spattered with dirty water.

Joey whizzed by, laughing loudly.

"He *is* a mean fellow," Tom said in disgust.

He pulled a big handkerchief from his pocket and gave it to Pam to wipe off the mud.

The unpleasant incident was forgotten as they reached the ice cream store. The children had fun choosing an assortment of flavors. They decided not to eat the ice cream there but to take it home. Laughing and skipping, the Hollisters started back with their new friend.

Darkness was coming over Shoreham and the street lights blinked on. As Pam and Pete walked along, a little behind the others, a slight sound made Pam glance over her shoulder. She noticed a strange man, of average size, who seemed to be very interested in them.

"Pete," she whispered, touching her brother's arm, "do you know that fellow?"

The boy turned his head, but not in time. The man had stepped into the shadow of a tree.

"I have a feeling he was following us," Pam said, worried. "But why?"

Pete shrugged. "He's gone now anyway," he said, and he and Pam caught up to the others.

Back at the Hollister house everyone had heaping plates of ice cream. While eating, the family asked Tom King to tell them something more about the mystery, and Pam added:

"I wish there were more clues to help solve it."

The young man glanced down and fingered an unusual tie clip he wore. A mass of tiny white crisscrossed logs was set in a gold bar. "This might be another clue."

"How?" Pete asked quickly.

"I had one of Grandmother Kalua's earrings set in this clip."

"It looks like coral," Mrs. Hollister remarked.

"You're right," Tom said, "from Hawaiian waters."

"But how is it a clue?" Ricky persisted, finishing the last spoonful of his ice cream.

"The mate to this earring was given by my grandparents to the clipper ship captain who married them," Tom replied. "If I could find that other earring, it might help me."

The Hollisters thought so too. Pam silently resolved to remember every detail of it.

Presently the children went to bed and Tom was shown to the guest room. The next morning Mr. Hollister offered to drive Tom to the repair shop to get his car. The four older children begged to go along, so he dropped them all off at the garage on his way to *The Trading Post.*

"Oh, there's my car," said Tom, and, followed by the children, hurried over to the small sedan.

He was pleased to find that the dents in the hood had been straightened out and that both doors opened properly.

"A fine job," he commented to the mechanic. But the next moment he let out a startled cry. "My brief case! It's gone!"

CHAPTER 4

FINDERS KEEPERS

A LOOK of dismay came over Tom King's face when the garage mechanic said he had not seen the brief case.

"It was on the seat yesterday," the Hawaiian said. "My brief case must have been stolen."

"Oh dear!" Pam cried out. "Your wonderful clue of the ship sketches is gone!"

Tom frowned. "Yes. I must find the case."

Just then another man wearing khaki overalls approached them, wiping his hands on a rag.

"I guess you're Mr. King," he said to Tom. "My name's Sampson. We fixed your car just as Officer Cal directed us to. Is something wrong?"

"You did an excellent job," Tom replied. "But I can't find a brown leather brief case I left in the car."

"I didn't see one inside," Mr. Sampson said, looking puzzled.

"Could someone have stolen it from here last night?" Pete asked.

"No, I'm certain of that," came the reply. "My night crew was on the job and no strangers could get in here without being seen."

"Well, let's look some more," Tom King said. "Perhaps I left it in the trunk."

But a thorough search of the car revealed no sign of the missing brief case.

Suddenly Pete snapped his fingers. "Crickets! I've got it! Remember the door of the car was hanging open?"

"So it was," Mr. Sampson said. "We fixed it up okay though."

"The brief case might have dropped out while the car was being towed here," Pete continued.

Both Tom and Sampson agreed that this was a possibility. "But where?" Tom asked anxiously. "It's some distance between your home on Shoreham Road and this garage."

Pam immediately suggested that they search along the route which the tow truck had taken and asked Mr. Sampson which way he had come after picking up Tom's sedan.

"Well, let's see," he said, tucking the rag into his back pocket. "Starting at Shoreham Road, we went south to Franklin Avenue, then right to Essex Street, then another right-hand turn along Broad Boulevard direct to the shop here."

"How far is that?" Tom King asked.

"About two miles," Pete put in.

"Pam, your idea's a good one. We'll search every inch of the route," Tom said determinedly.

The children waited while he paid his repair bill, then they all drove off in his car. With the children's help, he followed the route Sampson had mentioned, but did not see the brief case. When they reached home, Tom looked tired and discouraged.

Pam, noticing this, said kindly, "Why don't you wait here? Pete, Holly, Ricky, and I can take our bikes and search the ground from here to the garage."

"And we'll ask everybody we meet," Pete added. The young man thanked them, admitting that his head was beginning to ache again.

"I'll show you White Nose, our cat, and her kittens," Sue said, taking Tom by the hand.

Quickly getting their bicycles out of the garage, the other Hollister children set off on a hunt for the missing brief case.

"Let's search in twos," Pete suggested as they rode along. "Holly and I will take this side of the street while Pam and Ricky look along the other."

This was agreed. "In that way we shouldn't miss anything," Pam approved.

"Let's go! But ride slowly," Pete cautioned.

Litter tossed about by the storm the day before lay strewn against the curb on either side of the street. The riders, engrossed in their search, skirted around the leaves and fallen branches, and occasional patches of mud.

Coming to the Hunters' home, they saw Jeff and Ann playing hopscotch on the sidewalk.

When asked whether they had seen the missing brief case, both children said no, but they would be on the lookout for it. Soon the Hollisters were at Franklin Avenue, where they made a left turn.

"Here comes Dave Mead!" Pete said. "Maybe he can help us."

Dave also was riding his bike. He was twelve years old, had tousled hair, and was in Pete's class at school. The boys were good friends.

"Hi there!" Dave shouted. "You having a bicycle parade?"

"We're hunting for a lost brief case," Pam said.

"Detective work again, eh?" Dave teased. But he greatly admired his Hollister friends' ability to solve mysteries.

"That's right," Pete replied. "Did you see anything of a brown brief case?"

Dave shook his head, and the Hollisters continued along Franklin Avenue.

All at once Ricky called out, "I see it! I see it! Look over there!"

Up ahead on the right side of the road was a brown object. It was crushed against the curb and half covered with gravel and leaves.

Putting on a burst of speed, Pete was the first to reach it. He kicked aside the leaves and then uttered a sigh of disappointment.

"Only a brown shopping bag!" he said.

"Yikes!" Ricky exclaimed. "I thought sure we'd found it!"

Eyes darting here and there, the children turned the corner into Essex Street.

Halfway up the block a girl about Holly's age came tearing along the sidewalk on roller skates, her arms swinging from side to side like a windmill.

"That's Donna Martin!" Holly exclaimed. "Let's ask her."

Donna, seven years old, was Holly's classmate and best friend. She was a plump little girl with a dimple in each cheek. When Donna saw the Hollisters she tried to stop quickly, but lost her balance, falling forward and tumbling to the sidewalk. Ricky jumped off his bike and helped her up.

"Oh, I skinned my other knee this time," Donna said, puckering the corners of her mouth. Then in the same breath she asked, "Where are you going?"

Pete told the little girl about the missing brief case and asked her if she had seen it.

Donna put a finger to her chubby chin and lifted her eyes as if in deep thought. "Where was it lost?" she asked.

"Somewhere between our house and Broad Boulevard," Pam told her.

"Well, I saw a boy pick up something on Franklin last night," Donna said.

38

"What was it?" asked Ricky.

"I couldn't tell, 'cause it was getting dark," Donna said. "But he put it under his arm and hurried off as if it was real important."

"Who was the boy?" Pete wanted to know.

"I thought at first it was you," Donna replied. "But then I saw it wasn't. This boy was bigger."

The Hollisters looked at one another and Holly ventured, "Was it Joey Brill, maybe?"

Her little friend nodded slowly. "It did look like him, but the boy started running the other way so I couldn't see his face."

"Let's go see Joey Brill, anyway," Holly said, "and find out for sure."

The children thanked Donna, who promised to let them know if she should come across the brief case, and skated off. Then, pedaling rapidly, the Hollisters headed for the Brill home.

Reaching it, they found Joey on the front lawn. He was busy collecting night crawlers which had been flooded out of their underground homes by the heavy rain. As he picked up the worms, he dropped them into a tin can.

"Hi, Joey!" Pete called. The children parked their bikes at the curb in front of the house and walked over.

"Don't bother me," Joey said rudely, with hardly a glance. "I'm going fishing."

"Joey, we'd like to ask you——" Pam began, but the bully cut her off sharply.

39

"You Hollister pests—go somewhere else with your silly questions!" Joey scowled blackly at the girl.

Pete was growing angry at Joey's remarks, but he said as calmly as he could, "This is very important. We want to ask you a few questions about a missing brief case."

Joey jerked his head up. "What?" Then, without waiting for an answer, he said quickly, "No, I didn't see any brief case," and began digging furiously for worms.

The boy's manner indicated to the Hollisters that he might know more about Tom King's lost case than he would admit.

"Didn't you pick up something in the road last night?" Pete pressed.

Joey sprang up straight. "I wasn't in Franklin Avenue then," he stammered hastily.

"Nobody said you were," Ricky shot back.

At once Joey realized that he had fallen into a trap of his own making. His face grew red.

"Well, what if I did find an old beat-up brief case!" he cried out. "It's none of your business."

"So you did find it!" Holly shook an accusing finger at the bully.

"All right! All right! But what's that got to do with you?" the boy demanded.

"It belongs to a friend of ours," Pete said sternly. "And the brief case is very valuable to him. So give it to us, and we'll return it to him."

"We want to ask you a few questions."

"Ha-ha," Joey sneered, slipping two fingers into his worm can. "Finders keepers, that's what I say."

"That's not right!" Holly blurted. "Give us the brief case, Joey. It's not yours."

"Oh yeah?" With that, the bully took a worm out of the can and threw it straight at Holly. It hit her on the side of the neck, where it clung.

The girl let out a little shriek as she pulled the worm from her neck and flung it onto the ground. This was too much for Pete. He sprang forward and knocked the can out of Joey's hand.

Furious, the bully swung his right fist and cracked Pete on the jaw. Pete winced but returned a hard blow to Joey's nose. Then the boys grappled, falling to the ground and rolling over and over on the damp grass.

The noise attracted Mrs. Brill, who came rushing out of the house to see what the commotion was about. "Stop that immediately!" she cried, going over to separate the two boys. Then she added, "Oh, Joey, I wish you and the Hollisters wouldn't fight so much."

"He found a brief case which belongs to a friend of ours and he won't return it," Pam said.

"How do I know it's their friend's?" Joey scowled.

Quickly Pam explained to Mrs. Brill what had happened. "If the name Tom King is in the brief case," she concluded, "it belongs to the man at our house."

When Mrs. Brill asked her son about the brief case, he maintained a sulky silence at first, then responded with, "Oh, all right, it does say Tom King on the flap of the brief case."

"Then go get it right away," his mother said.

The boy shuffled into the house and returned a few minutes later with a brown leather brief case. "I was going to use it for my fishing tackle," he grumbled.

Mrs. Brill went into the house as Joey reluctantly handed the case over to Pete Hollister. He opened it quickly and looked inside. It was empty!

"Say, something's wrong here!" Pete exclaimed.

"What do you mean?" Joey demanded, glaring.

"There were some valuable sketches in this case. What did you do with them, Joey?"

"Oh, those!" Joey snorted. "They were just some drawings of an old ship."

"That's what's so valuable!" Pam cried. "Where did you put them?"

As the Hollisters looked on aghast, Joey pointed to a trash can at the curb. "I threw them in there," he said with a shrug.

"Oh no!" Pam wailed. "They're probably ruined!"

"And here come the trash collectors!" Ricky shouted.

43

CHAPTER 5

THE FLYING CLOUD

RICKY was right. Down the street rumbled a large disposal truck. It stopped before a house several doors away from Joey Brill's home. The man began emptying two cans standing at the curb.

Pete sprang into action. "We must get Tom's drawings even if they're ruined," he said, and raced to the container which held them. Yanking off the cover, he saw a roll of papers wedged up against the rim of the can. Pete reached in and pulled them out.

Joey walked over and said, "Those are the ones all right. But I can't see anything so great about them."

Pete unrolled the papers as the others looked on, revealing three beautiful sketches of a clipper ship.

"Hurray, hurray! We found them!" Ricky shouted while Holly jumped up and down with excitement.

"Now Tom King can look for his inheritance!" Holly said gleefully.

"Look for—what?" Joey asked.

"Never mind." Pam spoke up quickly. "It's nothing you'd be interested in."

"Aw, you Hollister kids are crazy anyhow!" Joey said scornfully. "Always making up stories."

Pete and Pam paid no attention to this, but examined the sketches again. They were damp around the edges, but fortunately had not been damaged otherwise.

The Hollisters mounted their bikes immediately and started off. Joey trotted along beside them for a while. "You kids think you're so smart. You just wait and see. I'll get back at you!"

The cyclists did not bother answering. Instead they pedaled faster until Joey was left behind. Upon arriving home, they found Tom King and Sue in the yard with White Nose, the cat, and her five kittens. The mother cat was pure black except for her white nose. One of her kittens, entirely black, was called Midnight. A pure white one was named Snowball. Tutti-Frutti was of mixed color, Smoky was gray, and the fifth kitten was called Cuddly because she was the smallest and most affectionate. Sue had put her wooden dollhouse in the sand box. Each kitten was perched in one of the rooms.

"We found the brief case!" Pete shouted, dropping his bike onto the lawn and dashing over to their guest.

"You did?" Tom cried, his face beaming. "Good!"

He took the brief case from Pete and, opening it, lifted out the three sketches. "How can I ever

"We found the brief case!"

thank you children?" he said, looking at them gratefully.

"We're just glad to help you," Pete said. Then he and the others told about their search and the tussle with Joey, stopped by Mrs. Brill.

The Hawaiian laughed at the last part, then said, "Now I can visit Mr. Sparr. Would you children like to go with me?"

"You bet!" Ricky said eagerly.

"Good!" Tom King said with a grin, adding that he felt entirely recovered. "Sue's stories about your pets were better than any medicine. I understand that you have a burro named Domingo, too."

"That's right," Pete said. "He's at our cousins' for a few weeks."

They all hurried into the house to tell Mrs. Hollister about the good luck they had had and to let her know they were going to call on Mr. Sparr.

"Fine, but you'd better have lunch first," she said.

After eating meat and cheese sandwiches, apples, and drinking glasses of milk, everyone got ready to leave. Mrs. Hollister suggested that Sue remain with her to help make an apple pie for supper.

"And may I have some of the dough to make special little cookies?" Sue asked. "For White Nose and the kittens," she explained.

Her mother smiled. "Yes, dear."

The other children climbed into Tom's car and drove toward Mr. Sparr's home. The Hollisters had known the retired seaman from the time they had put on a pirate show in their back yard. The good-natured old sailor had come to see it and quickly became firm friends with the family.

"There's the house," Pete said. "It's a real old one. See the date on the cornerstone: 1825."

Tom stopped the car and everyone got out. Ricky led the way up the steps and knocked on the screen door. Immediately an old man in sailor's clothes appeared. His spectacles were pushed up over his wrinkled forehead.

"Why, the Happy Hollisters!" he said heartily. "How are you? Welcome aboard!"

Pete introduced Tom King, and Mr. Sparr invited them all inside. "Haven't had such a treat since the full moon," he chuckled.

The Hollisters never tired of visiting the old seaman because of his funny remarks, and because his large living room was filled with souvenirs from ships—lanterns, anchors, chains, and even a foghorn. Three wooden models of sailing ships on the mantel were Mr. Sparr's special pride.

"Well, what can I do for you today?" the old man asked after his visitors had taken seats. "Are you looking for an anchor or an old sea horse?"

"Mr. King wants you to help solve a mystery for him," Pam said, whereupon the Islander

48

opened his brief case and took out the sketches.

"Take a look at these, if you will," he requested.

Mr. Sparr searched through all his pockets for his spectacles but could not find them.

Pam giggled. "You have them on already, Mr. Sparr."

"So I do!" the old sailor said with a chuckle as he pulled the glasses down from his forehead.

After he had adjusted them he looked at the three drawings.

"Marvelous! Wonderful!" he exclaimed. "I've never seen such detailed drawings of a clipper ship in all my life. And what is the name of this beauty?"

"That's what I would like to find out," Tom King said, and unfolded the story of his visit to the United States.

When he finished speaking, Mr. Sparr studied the sketches carefully. Finally he said, "I'm sorry, but I can't identify this ship, even though my grandfather sailed on clippers many years ago and told me all about them." Then he scratched his head and frowned as he placed a gnarled finger on the deck plan of the clipper.

"Hm! Most unusual," he remarked. "The three lifeboats are aft instead of for'ard. I don't recall any other ship having this arrangement."

"It might be a good clue," Pete suggested.

"You're right. It may help in identifying this

49

clipper," Mr. Sparr said. "And, by the way, there's something I'd advise you to do, Mr. King."

"What's that?"

"Have a photostat made of these drawings just in case you should ever lose them," the old seaman replied.

"What's a photostat?" Holly piped up, and Mr. Sparr explained it meant taking a picture of the sketches.

Tom and the Hollisters thought this an excellent idea, and the Hawaiian said he would have it done immediately. Then he asked:

"Mr. Sparr, could you suggest any place I might go to find out the name of this ship?"

The sailor took off his glasses and tapped them against his knee. "I'd suggest you see Mr. Dooley, curator of the Marine Museum at Orient Harbor."

"In Massachusetts?" Pam asked.

"That's right," the old man replied. "Orient Harbor has one of the best museums in the world. From that port the famous clippers set sail for California and across the Pacific in olden times."

"Thank you," said Tom, then asked Mr. Sparr about the ship models on the mantel.

"The middle one is the *Flying Cloud*," Mr. Sparr replied. "I made her myself while I was on a trip to Australia."

He rose and walked across to the mantel, then carefully lifted the model to a nearby table. As the children crowded around, Mr. Sparr said:

"This clipper, the *Flying Cloud*, was built in East Boston. A real beauty, too."

"How large was she?" Pete asked.

"Exactly 1783 tons register," Mr. Sparr said proudly. "She measured 225 feet long and 40 feet 8 inches wide." Then he added, with a flourish of his hand, "Depth 21 feet 6 inches, with 20 inches' dead rise at half floor."

"Yikes! You know all about her, don't you?" Ricky said.

"And was she a mile high?" Holly put in.

"Nearly so," Mr. Sparr said with a chuckle. "Her main yard was 82 feet and her mainmast 88 feet in length. She was commanded by Captain Josiah Perkins Cressy, who was born in Marblehead in 1814."

The old seaman's acquaintance with clippers and the men who sailed them intrigued the Hollisters. As they stood admiring the graceful lines of the ship model, Ricky asked about her many sails.

Mr. Sparr explained that each of the three masts carried five different sails. The foremast had a foresail, a topsail, a topgallant sail, a royal and a skysail.

"And how about this middle one?" Pam asked, pointing to the tallest mast.

"That's the mainmast," Mr. Sparr said. "And at the bottom is the mainsail."

Then he pointed out the mast at the stern of

the ship, called the mizzenmast. Its sails were the spanker, topsail, topgallant, royal, and skysail.

"Crickets!" Pete exclaimed. "A sea captain would have to be pretty smart to know all the sails and the ropes that go with them."

"Now how would you like to take this model home to study?" Mr. Sparr asked the Hollisters.

"Yikes! That would be great!" Ricky exclaimed. "Say, Pete, couldn't we remodel our rowboat to look like the *Flying Cloud*?"

"Sure, let's try it," his brother replied with enthusiasm.

"I'll carry it home," Holly offered, starting to pick up the clipper model. In her eagerness she let the stern slip through her fingers and it hit the table with a bang!

"Oh!" Mr. Sparr exclaimed, putting his hands over his eyes. He took them away slowly and looked at his model. Then he grinned. "Nothing broken. But please take good care of this. And, for goodness' sake, keep it away from water."

"Why?" Ricky asked.

The old sailor explained that the glue which held the model together might be dissolved by moisture.

"Okay," Pete promised, "we'll be sure to keep the *Flying Cloud* dry. And I'd better carry it, Holly."

"Thanks for the information you gave me,"

Tom King said. "I'll get in touch with Mr. Dooley."

"Perhaps I'll contact him myself," the old seaman murmured.

With Pete carrying the ship model, Tom and the children left Mr. Sparr's home.

"Tom, why don't you go right now and have the copies of your sketches made?" Pam suggested. "We can walk home. It's not far."

"All right," he said, and drove off toward the center of town, where Pete had given him the address of a photostat shop.

The Hollisters had not gone more than a block when Joey Brill rode up on his bike. "I've been looking for you," he told them.

"Did you bring your worms with you?" Ricky asked.

Joey ignored the gibe. "I came to tell you something."

"Go ahead," Pete invited.

"It's about White Nose, your cat," Joey said.

"What's the matter with her?" Pam asked a little anxiously.

"She's up a tree—'way up."

"Where?" the Hollisters chorused.

"Down the street." Joey pointed. "She's so high that she can't get down. I'll show you."

"Oh, hurry!" Pam cried. "We must help White Nose!"

CHAPTER 6

RICKY'S PRANK

WHITE NOSE had the unfortunate habit of climbing to the top of tall trees and being afraid to come down by herself. Twice Pete had had to climb up and rescue her.

"Oh dear, I hope White Nose isn't out on the end of a shaky branch," Pam said worriedly as they hurried down the street after Joey, who rode fast.

"She's so high you can hardly see her," he said over his shoulder, trying to conceal a smirk.

Presently the group came to a big house set back on a broad lawn. Off to the side was a garage and close by towered a huge oak tree.

"She's in that tree there," Joey said, pointing.

The Hollisters could not see White Nose from where they were standing, so all of them walked under the tree and looked up through its spreading branches. The mother cat's dark fur might not be spotted easily from below.

"I can't see her," Pete called to Joey, who still stood on the sidewalk astride his bike. "Are you sure she's up there?"

The boy did not answer. Just then the topmost branches of the tree began to shake violently and raindrops which were still on the leaves pelted down on the Hollisters.

"What's going on?" Pete demanded, running away.

"Ha, ha, fooled you this time!" Joey said, doubling over with laughter.

"Hey! I see what happened," Ricky called out. "There's a rope tied to the top limb and somebody's pulling the other end of it."

By this time all the children had dashed from under the tree. They were wet, but worst of all, so was the precious ship model which Pete held in his hands.

Just then, Will Wilson, a friend of Joey's, poked his head up over the ridge of the garage roof. Will had many times helped Joey in mischief-making and annoying the Hollisters.

"Your old cat isn't in the tree at all," he cried gleefully. "We just wanted to give you a shower."

"Yeah, you Hollisters are all wet anyhow," Joey taunted from the sidewalk, then hopped on his bike and sped off.

"If you only knew where we got the rope!" Will chortled.

He shinned down the garage water spout and jumped onto his bike, which was concealed behind a nearby hedge.

Pam and Holly wiped raindrops from their eyes and hair, glad that White Nose had not been trapped after all.

Pete, however, was too concerned about the clipper ship model to chase after the bullies at the moment. "I hope it's not ruined," he said.

He looked worriedly at Mr. Sparr's prized model. Its sails were damp, and its hull covered with drops of water. Would the ship come apart?

"Maybe you can wipe it dry before it comes to any harm," Holly suggested. "Here's a clean handkerchief."

Pete took it and very carefully tried to sop up the moisture on the tiny vessel. But, gentle as he was, the two top yardarms fell away from the mainmast and left the skysail and royal sail dangling.

"Now we've really done it!" Pete groaned.

"Maybe we can mend it at home," Ricky said hopefully as they started off.

When Mrs. Hollister heard what had happened, she said, "It's too bad, but I'm sure the ship model can be repaired. Leave it on the living-room table until your father comes home. He may know what to do."

Pete's face brightened. "That gives me an idea," he declared. "Dad has waterproof glue at *The Trading Post.*"

Ricky offered to go get some and hurried off. He had just returned when Tom King's car turned into the driveway. In a few minutes the young man was showing the Hollisters the photostats of the clipper sketches.

Raindrops pelted down on the Hollisters.

"These prints are keen!" Pete said. "Now if you lose one set, you'll have the other."

"That's right. But, to be on the safe side, I shouldn't carry both around with me," the Hawaiian remarked. "Suppose," he added, "I leave the photostats with you. If I ever want them I can let you know."

"We'll do our best to take good care of them," Mrs. Hollister said, and immediately placed the photostats in the drawer of a writing desk.

"I'm sure you will," Tom replied. "And now I think I'll have to say good-by. I'd like to get to Orient Harbor tomorrow and see Mr. Dooley at the museum there."

"Please, can't you stay to supper?" Holly begged, and her mother said, "We'll eat early so you can drive partway to Orient Harbor before dark."

Tom accepted gladly, saying that he would be delighted to spend a few hours more with the Happy Hollisters.

"Maybe you can help us repair the *Flying Cloud*," Holly suggested, and told him of the mishap to the clipper model.

"I'll be glad to," Tom replied. "First we'll need a pair of tweezers."

Holly ran upstairs and got one. Now Tom directed Pete to hold the yardarms in place with the tweezers.

"Next comes the glue," he said, and Ricky handed over the bottle.

Tom started applying the waterproof glue to the tiny sections. "This is very tricky," he commented as he worked.

"It's going to look just as good as new!" Pam exclaimed in delight.

Holly had pulled up a chair and, after tossing her pigtails over the back of it, watched intently as Tom worked with skillful fingers.

"Will you hold the glue bottle, Ricky?" the Hawaiian asked. "I may need a little more in a moment."

Ricky stepped back a few paces while all eyes were intent upon the repair job.

"There! That does it!" Tom said as Pete let go of the yardarms. They were firmly in place. The glue was not only strong and waterproof, but set quickly as well.

"We sell nothing but the best at *The Trading Post*," Pam said with a wink.

Holly got up from her chair to take a closer look at the *Flying Cloud*. Instantly she cried out, "Ow!"

"What's the matter?" Pam asked.

"My pigtails are stuck!" The ends clung to the back of her chair like steel to a magnet.

"How did that happen?" Pete cried, and went to examine the tip end of her braids. "Crickets!" he cried. "They're glued to the wood!"

Holly, alarmed, tugged at her pigtails. But they would not come loose.

Just then Mrs. Hollister, attracted by the commotion, came from the kitchen. "Goodness!" she exclaimed. "Now who did that?" The children's mother looked around, then said, "All I need is one guess."

She gazed directly at Ricky, who had set the glue bottle on the table. The red-haired boy said nothing and evaded his mother's eyes.

"Ricky!" Mrs. Hollister's voice grew sterner. "Did you do this, Son?"

"I—I can't tell a lie," Ricky replied finally, trying to look very serious. "I did it with *The Trading Post's* super-special glue."

"You meanie!" Holly cried.

She wriggled this way and that, trying to free her pigtails, but they remained fast.

"I can't go around dragging this chair all my life!" she said, frowning. The tugging pulled her hair and hurt a bit.

"I'll get some hot water. That will soften the glue," Mrs. Hollister offered.

"You can't—it's waterproof," Pete reminded her.

"I'm sorry, Holly," Ricky said. "I didn't think it would stick your hair that tight."

"Well, get me loose," his sister demanded pettishly.

Everyone took a turn trying to yank the braids

loose from the back of the chair, but each time Holly yelled that it hurt.

Tom King, meanwhile, had been looking on without a word. His face was serious, but his brown eyes held an amused glint. Now he stepped forward and said, "I'm afraid there's only one thing to do. Use scissors."

Mrs. Hollister nodded sadly. "I'm afraid so, too," she agreed.

"What! Cut off her head?" Pete asked, grinning.

"It's not that funny," Pam reproved him.

"Tom is right," Mrs. Hollister said. "We'll have to cut an inch off each pigtail. Pam, will you please get the scissors for me?" Turning to Ricky, she added, "Don't you ever do that again."

"I promise on my honor," the boy said, holding up two fingers.

In a moment Pam returned with the scissors. *Snip, snip!* And Holly was free again.

When Mr. Hollister came home and everyone sat down to supper, he asked to hear the day's adventures of his family. One by one they reported their views. At the end he said he was pleased to hear that the clipper model had been fixed. Then Mr. Hollister turned to Ricky.

"To make up for your prank," he said, "I want you to take the chair to the garage, scrape the hair from it, and after that touch it up with stain and varnish."

Ricky gulped but nodded, and his brother and sisters began to laugh.

"My hair was getting too long anyhow," said Holly, patting her shortened pigtails.

Directly after the meal Tom got his suitcase and the family accompanied him to the car. Shaking hands with all the Hollisters, he thanked them for their hospitality and voiced the hope that he would see them again someday.

"Please let us know if you solve your inheritance mystery," Pam said.

"I will," he promised.

Sue declared she had something she wanted to whisper in Tom's ear. "It's a secret," she said.

When the young man bent over, she threw her arms around his neck and said, "Come back soon."

Tom chuckled. "I'll try. You're as sweet as a Hawaiian pineapple."

After a chorus of good-bys, Tom got into his car and backed out of the driveway. The Hollister children ran to the street to wave as he turned and headed down Shoreham Road.

But he had gone only fifty yards or so when Pam cried out, "Look who's in the back seat!"

There was Zip, their collie, proudly looking out the rear window of Tom's car. The driver did not seem to know he was there.

"Zip's riding away to Massachusetts!" Holly shrieked. "He mustn't! He mustn't!"

CHAPTER 7

THE ROWBOAT CLIPPER

LED by Pete, the Hollister children raced down the street, crying out at the top of their lungs.

"Stop, Tom! Stop!"

"Don't take our dog!"

Suddenly the automobile came to a halt. Then, to the children's relief, it began to back up.

"I guess Zip wanted to be an old sea dog," Pete chuckled.

The children met Tom halfway down the block and Ricky opened the right-hand door. Zip jumped out.

"What were you trying to do, old fellow?" Pete asked. "Be a stowaway?"

Tom King laughed. "Zip certainly gave me a surprise. How did he get in?"

No one knew, but Pam suggested that he must have slipped in unnoticed, after Tom's suitcase had been placed in the car, and gone to sleep on the floor.

"Zip likes you," Holly said, "and wanted to go to Orient Harbor with you." The girl added wistfully, "So do I."

"Perhaps all of you will have a chance to

come," Tom said, winking at the children. "I'll be there for a while."

Saying good-by once more, Tom got back into the car. With a wave of his hand, he started off.

Zip whimpered a little as the automobile turned the corner and disappeared. But he soon regained his usual peppy spirit, bounding around the children as they walked back toward their home.

"We'll start to make our rowboat clipper tomorrow," Pete told Ricky.

"What can Holly and I do?" Pam asked him.

"You can help make the sails," her brother said.

"Okay, that'll be the girls' project," Pam agreed.

After breakfast next morning the children ran across the back lawn to the family's dock, where the rowboat was tied up. Then work began in earnest. Using Mr. Sparr's model of the *Flying Cloud* as a pattern, Pete and Ricky decided to start at the front.

"The bowsprit extends a good ways over the bow," Pete said. "What can we use to make one?"

Ricky suggested a broken clothes pole in the garage and hurried to get it.

"That'll be neat," Pete said when his brother returned. "I'll brace it on both sides of the bow like this." He held the pole in place with two pieces of lumber he had asked Ricky to bring. Then he proceeded to cut them to the right length and hammered them into place.

"Yikes! It begins to look keen!" Ricky said gleefully. "What do we do next, Pete?"

"Set up the masts," came the reply.

After studying the model boat a little more, the boys decided they would bore holes in the three seats of the rowboat.

"We can fit the poles right into them," Pete said.

"But where are you going to get the poles?" Ricky asked. "We haven't any long enough."

"Why not buy them at a lumberyard?" Pam suggested. "We can ride our bikes there and can carry the poles home together."

It was decided that Ricky should stay at the dock to drill the holes for the mast while Pete and Pam went to purchase the wood.

"Don't forget that we need rope for the rigging, too," Ricky said.

"We'll get it at The Trading Post," Pam said. "Let's go there first."

She and Pete rode their bikes to The Trading Post, parking them at the back of the building. They always liked to visit their father's store, for it contained a fascinating variety of hardware. And, besides, Mr. Hollister sold the most up-to-date toys and sports equipment. Now the

65

children went in the rear entrance and walked up a long aisle toward the front of the store.

"Hi there!" an elderly man greeted them.

"Hello, Tinker," they answered. Tinker, a tall, thin fellow with a kindly face, had been hired by Mr. Hollister shortly after opening The Trading Post.

"How's business today?" Pete asked him with a wink.

"Lively as the Hollisters," the man replied, smiling. "Your father just left for a business club luncheon."

As Tinker went off to wait on a customer, another clerk greeted the children. He was short, stocky, and had black hair. His high cheekbones and reddish-tan complexion plainly stamped him as an Indian.

"Indy," Pam said, calling him by his nickname, "we'd like to buy some rope."

"Going to make some lariats?" he asked, grinning.

"No, we want it for rigging on our clipper ship," Pete replied, and explained their project.

"I don't know much about ships," Indy replied. "We don't hear much about sea life in the desert, where I lived."

Indy Roades had come originally from the West. He had become acquainted with the Hollisters when he helped the children solve a mystery, and Mr. Hollister had offered him a job in the store.

"I think we have just what you need," the Indian said, walking over to one side of the store where a big spool of rope lay on the floor. "This is very light clothesline rope."

"That's dandy," Pete said. "I think a hundred feet will be enough."

"And we'll wait on customers to earn it, too," Pam promised.

As Indy reeled the rope from the spool, he remarked, "Someone you know bought the same kind of rope here yesterday."

"Who?" asked Pete.

"Will Wilson."

"So that's where he got it!" Pam said.

She told their Indian friend about the oak tree incident. He agreed it was a very mischievous trick and was glad the model of the *Flying Cloud* had not been ruined. Then, as he looped a coil around the hank of rope, Indy said, "Look. There comes a customer you'd like to wait on, I'm sure."

Pete and Pam wheeled about to see Will Wilson himself coming through the front entrance. He had a large paper bag in his hand.

"I'll wait on him!" Pete said grimly.

"But try to be polite," his sister warned. "Don't forget he's still a customer of Dad's."

Pete walked briskly up to Will Wilson. When

67

the bully saw him, he was so surprised he nearly dropped the paper bag.

"May I help you?" Pete asked.

"Why—a—yeah—I mean—a——" Will stammered, obviously flustered by the Hollisters' presence.

"Don't get upset," Pete said coolly. "We're always glad to oblige our customers."

"I came to return something," Will said finally, flushing.

"What is it?" Pete asked, extending a hand to take the bag.

"I'd rather not show you now," Will protested.

"If something is wrong with our merchandise, we'll make an exchange," Pete said.

He took the parcel from the other boy and opened it. Inside were several feet of rope!

"Do you wish to return this?" Pete asked, without changing his calm expression.

"Well—yes, if I can," Will said.

"What's wrong with it?"

"It was too short."

Pete knew Will was lying. This was the same rope he had purchased to tie to the top of the oak tree!

Will shifted uneasily from one foot to the other as Pete continued, "Perhaps you'd like a longer piece of rope, Will?"

"I just want my money back," the boy said sullenly.

"I came to return something," Will said, flushing.

Pete realized this was an unfair request. But he had often heard his father say that a customer is always right and must be treated courteously. Keeping this in mind, Pete asked Will to wait and went to the rear of the store to speak to Pam. After whispering something to her, he returned.

"How much did you pay for the rope, Will?"

"Forty cents."

"Go to the back of the store and get the money from Pam."

Will Wilson looked surprised at the ease with which he was getting away with returning the used piece of rope. He walked back to where Pam was standing near the rear door.

"Pete says to give me forty cents," Will said curtly.

Pam went to a nearby cash register and got the money. Handing it to Will, she said, "Why don't you go out the back door? It's quicker."

The bully appeared amazed at the polite treatment he was receiving.

"Thanks," he stammered, and walked out.

But the minute he stepped to the yard, Will gave a startled cry. "I thought you were——"

"No, I'm outside now!" came Pete's voice as cold as steel. He had run out the front entrance and down the side driveway, meeting Will at the back.

"Here's something I forgot to give you!" Pete said.

Thump! He hit Will on the chest. This unexpected turn of events startled the bully so much that he dashed away without putting up a fight.

When Pete re-entered the store, Pam, Tinker, and Indy had a good chuckle over what had happened.

"Served him right," Tinker chortled.

The children worked in the store almost an hour to earn the money for their purchase. Then, as they were about to leave, Tinker said, "I knew there was something I wanted to find out from you."

"What is it?" Pam asked.

"Did you see the man who was asking about your house guest?"

"Why, no. Who was he?"

"I don't know his name," Tinker replied, "but he was here earlier in the day and wanted to know whether Tom King had left your place."

The children were excited. "What was his name? What did he look like?" Pete asked.

Tinker said the man had not given his name. He was of medium height, with a red face and thin blond hair. "The fellow wore a bright checkered sports jacket," Tinker concluded.

The Hollisters immediately wondered whether he might be the same man who had seemed to be following them two nights before from the ice cream store.

"If you see him again, Tinker, let us know," Pete said.

Taking the rope, he and Pam left the store. They hopped on their bikes again and headed for the lumberyard. It was located at the edge of town and comprised several long sheds, under which row after row of sweet-smelling, well-seasoned wood was stored.

As the dealer approached the children, Pete said they would like to purchase three long poles to use as masts for their clipper ship. The man looked so surprised Pete chuckled. "We're making one out of our rowboat," he explained.

"Oh, I get it," the dealer grinned, adding, "I think I have exactly the thing."

The Hollisters followed him to the end of a long shed. Here the man reached in and pulled out three long poles.

"These were ordered by a boy who wanted to build a sailboat," he said. "But the lad never showed up, so you can have them cheap."

Pete and Pam exchanged happy glances. Just what they wanted!

"Shall I deliver them for you?" the dealer asked. "They're pretty long to carry."

"I think we can take them on our bikes," Pete said. "I'll hold one end and Pam can ride behind me, holding the other."

"All right, if that's the way you want it," the man said.

After Pete had paid for the wood, he mounted his bike. Then he placed one end of each pole over his handlebars, two on one side of him, one on the other. Some fifteen feet behind him, Pam did the same with the other ends.

"I hope you make it all right," the lumber man said dubiously. "Be careful at the intersections."

As Pete and Pam started pedaling toward home, onlookers smiled to see the unusual-looking caravan.

"I feel like a hook-and-ladder driver!" Pete called back to his sister.

Everything went all right until the two children came to an intersection. In the distance Pete saw a car coming, but he called to Pam, "If we hurry we can make it all right."

But the car was coming faster than they thought and the children realized they could not get across the intersection without being hit.

"Pete, what'll we do?" Pam cried out.

CHAPTER 8

A DOLL FIGUREHEAD

THERE was only one thing for Pete and Pam to do to avoid a collision—drop the poles and steer for the side of the road. With the oncoming car only a few feet from them, its brakes screeching, the children hurled the long poles to the street and swerved their bikes to one side.

Bang! Bump! The car ran over the poles, missing the brother and sister by inches.

"Whew!" exclaimed Pete, and Pam was shaking from fright.

To their amazement, the car driver, instead of stopping to see if the children were all right, continued down the street at a fast clip.

"What an awful man!" Pam cried, then asked, "Are the poles damaged?"

"I don't think so," Pete replied, bending over to examine them. "They're hard wood."

"I have one clue about that speeding driver," Pete said. "He was wearing a bright checkered jacket."

"And I noticed his car had California license plates," Pam added. "Maybe he's the same man who came into *The Trading Post* and asked Tinker about Tom King," she mused.

74

"He might have been," Pete said. "Do you suppose he's been looking for Tom all the way from the West Coast?"

Pam thought this over, then said with a worried look, "Oh dear, I hope he's not trying to cause any trouble for Tom."

The children resolved to be on the alert for clues to the stranger's identity and ask the rest of the family to be also. They loaded the poles onto their bicycles and once more set out toward home. When the children arrived, they found Dave Mead helping Ricky make mast holes in the rowboat clipper.

"I think your clipper idea's terriffic!" Dave said enthusiastically.

As Pam and Pete took the poles and rope from their bicycles, Ricky exclaimed, "Those will make swell masts!"

The three boys set them in place. They fitted the holes perfectly. Next Pete braced the three poles with blocks attached to the floor of the boat.

"Next come the yardarms, and then the sails," Ricky said, standing back to admire the rakish look of the ship.

"There are some pieces of wood in the cellar that'll be good for making the yardarms," Pete said, and went to get them.

Pam suggested that she, Holly, and Sue start

making the sails. "I think Mother has some old sheets we can use."

When they asked her, she said that in the attic was a laundry bag full of discarded sheets.

"Help yourselves," she added, smiling.

The three sisters climbed the stairs to the attic. Under the eaves was the large white laundry bag. Pam dragged it to the center of the floor. Holly opened it and pulled out several sheets.

Meanwhile Sue had found a box of old toys and was rummaging through them. Presently she found an Indian doll which Pam had discarded.

As Holly glanced up and saw it, she exclaimed, "Oh, that would be a wonderful figurehead for our clipper ship!"

"What are figgerheads?" Sue asked.

Pam explained that they were wooden statues which were often attached to the bows of old-time clipper ships.

"Let's tell the boys our idea," Holly said.

"I have to get the measurements for the sails from Pete," said Pam, "so I'll go down with you." Sue remained in the attic to play.

The two older girls hurried downstairs with the old Indian doll.

"That'll be good!" Ricky exclaimed when the girls suggested the Indian figurehead.

"Let's tie it under the bowsprit," Pete suggested.

"We'll have to think up a good Indian name for our clipper ship," Pam mused, fastening the doll to the front of the rowboat with a heavy cord.

"Say, that looks super," Dave said admiringly.

"Sure does," Pete grinned, then suddenly looked around. "What's that noise?"

A tapping sound drew everyone's attention to the third-floor window. Sue was beckoning for them to come.

"I'll bet she found another old toy," Holly guessed. She cupped her hands. "We'll be up soon," she called.

After learning the measurements of the yardarms, Pam and Holly figured out how large to make the sails. Pam jotted the sizes down on a pad of paper, then she and her sister went back to the attic.

Sue was not there.

"Maybe she went downstairs again," Holly suggested.

The girls retraced their steps. They called and called, but no word from Sue.

"She couldn't just disappear," Pam insisted. "I wonder if she's in trouble."

"Do you suppose she's hiding in the secret stairway?" Holly asked.

When the Hollisters had come to live in Shoreham, they discovered a hidden stairway which led from the attic to the cellar. Pam and Holly now went to the basement, opened the door of

77

Pam fastened the doll to the front of the boat.

the secret stairway, and walked clear up to the attic. Sue was not to be found.

"If you're playing tricks, Sue, please don't, because we're worried," Pam called out.

Just then they heard a small *meow*. Instantly the two girls looked for White Nose or her kittens, but none of them was in sight. The *meow* came again, this time a little louder.

Suddenly Pam's and Holly's eyes fell on the white laundry bag. Something inside it wiggled!

Quietly the two girls, with a wink at each other, approached the bag. Then they grabbed it.

"So there you are, Sue!" Pam said.

The little girl poked her head out of the sack, her eyes sparkling with mischief. "Ha, ha, you couldn't find me!" she teased.

"What an imp you are!" Pam laughed.

She and Holly set to work on their sail-making. Carefully measuring the old sheets, they cut out the number of pieces that were needed. Sue begged to help. She was given a small pair of scissors to cut out the tiny skysails.

"This is more work than I thought," Holly sighed as she snipped at the material.

When all the sails were cut, Sue chirped, "Now we can put them on and go out in our clipper boat!"

"Not quite," Pam reminded her. "We have to hem the edges so they'll be strong."

The three girls gathered all the pieces of

material and took them downstairs to the sunroom, where Mrs. Hollister kept her sewing machine. With Holly and Sue standing by admiringly, Pam quickly put the hems in the sails.

As she was finishing, the front door bell rang. Holly ran to answer it.

"Oh, Mr. Sparr," she said, "come in."

As the old sailor entered the house, he seemed very excited. "I have news for you," he announced.

"Oh, tell us what it is," Pam said eagerly.

"Are the boys around? They'll want to hear it, too."

"I'll get them," Holly volunteered, and hurried out the back door.

In a moment she returned with her brothers and Dave Mead, who knew Mr. Sparr. As they gathered around the old man, he said, "Belay me for an old dolphin, but my curiosity got the better of me."

"What do you mean?" Pete asked.

"It's about that nice Hawaiian fellow," Mr. Sparr replied. "I got to thinkin' about him, so last night I telephoned my old friend Mr. Dooley direct."

"Did you tell him about Tom's drawings of the clipper ship?" Pam asked.

Mr. Sparr nodded. "Yep, I sure did."

"What did Mr. Dooley say?" Ricky asked excitedly.

"I was just comin' to that, Rick. I explained

80

about the lifeboats being aft instead of for'ard, and my old friend said he knew of a clipper like that."

"What was her name?" Pete cried, and the others waited breathlessly for the answer.

"The *Winged Chief*," said Mr. Sparr. "Mind you now, it might not have been the one. Mr. Dooley doesn't know for sure. But he told me if those old drawings do turn out to be of the *Winged Chief*, they're worth a good bit of money."

The Hollisters and Dave looked at one another, astonished. "Why would they be so valuable?" Pam asked.

"Seems a movie company wants to get hold of them," the old seaman said.

"Oh!" Pam exclaimed. "Won't Tom King be excited to learn that!"

"I hope he lets us know when he gets to Orient Harbor," Holly said. "I'd like to write him a letter."

Mr. Sparr suddenly said, "Oh, there's something else Mr. Dooley wanted me to pass along to you Hollisters."

"What's that?" Pete asked.

"When I told him you were keeping photostats of the sketches," the old man replied, "Mr. Dooley warned you to guard them very carefully."

81

CHAPTER 9

AN ICY BUMP

DAVE MEAD, as well as the Hollister children, was very impressed when he heard how valuable even the photostats of the old clipper ship sketches were. "It's a good thing Mr. Dooley warned you. It sounds as if somebody might try to steal them," he remarked.

Pam and Pete exchanged glances, the same thought crossing their minds. Could the reckless driver in the checkered jacket have something to do with the mystery?

Aloud Pam said, "We'd better pay attention to what Mr. Dooley said." She walked over to her mother's writing desk and tried the drawer in which the photostats had been put. It was locked. "They're in here," she said.

"Guess they'll be safe and sound, then," Mr. Sparr replied.

Before he left, the children invited him to see how work on the rowboat clipper was progressing.

"That's fine!" he said. "She's going to be swift and beautiful. Ought to be able to do twenty knots."

"Twenty knots?" Ricky piped up. "I don't see any knots."

Pete chuckled. "A knot is how fast a boat can go over water," he explained.

"Is that the same as twenty miles an hour?" Holly asked, and all eyes turned to Mr. Sparr for the answer.

"Well, almost," the old seaman said. He explained that the ancient Romans had established a land mile at approximately 4,845 feet, while a modern mile is 5,280 feet. A sea mile, or nautical mile, is 1/60th of a degree of latitude.

"Yikes!" Ricky blinked rapidly. "What does all that mean?"

The old fellow stroked his stubby beard. "Just to make it simple," he said, "a nautical mile is 6,080 feet, and it is measured in knots."

"How many knots is it across Pine Lake?" Dave Mead wanted to know.

"You only talk about knots when you mean speed," Mr. Sparr explained. "Distance is spoken of in nautical miles, and speed in knots, like twenty knots an hour."

"How many yeses in an hour?" asked Sue, who had a puzzled expression on her face.

Everyone laughed, and Pam said, "A knot is not an n-o-t," she spelled, "it's a k-n-o-t."

"Oh, like the ones in my shoelaces?" Sue asked.

Again the other children laughed, but they stopped when Mr. Sparr said, "That's exactly right. You see the name comes from the way sailors used to measure their speed. They dropped a piece of wood, or a log, over the stern into the water. A piece of light line was tied to it, and the line had knots in it at regular spaces. The sailor handling the log line would count how many knots went out in a certain time, and that would tell them their speed."

"I see," said Pete and Pam, but the others asked to have it repeated.

Finally they thought they understood and thanked Mr. Sparr for his information. The elderly seaman smiled. "All of you will be old salts by the time you finish building your rowboat clipper," he chuckled. Then he set off for his own house.

The Hollisters, assisted by Dave Mead, continued work on the ship. The girls brought out the finished sails.

"They look neat," Pete praised his sisters.

As Dave steadied the boat alongside the dock, Pete fitted the yardarms to the mizzenmast. Starting with the skysail yard, he worked his way down the pole until all of them were in place.

"Now for the braces," Pete said as he hopped onto the dock from the rowboat to pick up the coil of rope.

After studying the model of the *Flying Cloud*, Pete had learned that the braces were used to pull the sails from one position to another in order to catch the wind most advantageously.

Suddenly Dave said, "See who's coming down your driveway!"

Pete turned and his expression clouded. Joey Brill was pedaling his bicycle down a path toward them. He stopped a few feet away from the boys and got off.

"Oh, don't act so surprised," Joey said. "I heard all about Will Wilson returning the rope."

"I think you had some nerve to do that," Pete said, disgust in his voice.

"Don't look at me like that," Joey said. "It wasn't my idea."

Dave Mead exchanged glances with Pete, looked up at the sky, and started to whistle.

"Oh, you don't believe me, eh?" Joey said.

No one answered the question. Pete asked, "What do you want here?"

"Nothing. I just want to watch you build your clipper ship."

By this time Pam had finished hemming the last skysail and Sue proudly carried the three sails out to her brothers.

"They look neat!" Joey said, acting more polite than the Hollisters had seen him for many days.

"They're beautiful," Sue remarked. "Just like the ones on the *Flying Cloud*."

"What's that?" Joey asked.

"Our clipper ship model," Sue blurted out. "The one you got wet."

"I never did get a good look at it," Joey said.

"It's valuable!" Sue continued. "We have valuable sketches too, don't we, Pete?"

Her brother put a finger to his lips as a silent sign for his sister not to tell any more.

When Joey noticed this, he said, "All right. If it's a big secret, don't tell me. I want to see the *Flying Cloud* model."

At first Pete did not wish to show it to him, but when Joey begged, the Hollister boy said, "If you promise to take good care of it, I'll let you see the model."

"Sure, sure, I won't hurt it."

Pete went into the house and returned with Mr. Sparr's wonderful model of the old clipper ship.

"Um," said Joey, "not bad." He took it from Pete's hands and examined the miniature ship carefully.

"I'll bet this could make good time in the water," he said, moving toward the dockside.

"You mustn't put it in the water," Pete warned. "Here, give it back."

"Aw, let me sail it just once," Joey begged.

"No! The glue will come apart," Ricky warned him. "That's what happened before."

"Aw, just one minute in the water wouldn't hurt the old glue," Joey insisted.

"Come on, give it back," Pete demanded, reaching for the boat model.

86

Joey was always annoyed to be told what to do. Angrily he spun away from Pete. "I'm going to sail your old boat anyhow," he announced.

"You'd better not."

"Who's going to stop me?"

"I am!" Pete's eyes were flashing.

Dave Mead stepped up beside his friend. "If you have any trouble, Pete, I'll help you."

"Thanks, but I don't need any help," Pete said, and with a lightning grab got his hands on the boat. "Give it to me!"

"You'd think your old boat was made of gold," Joey taunted.

With that, he shoved the model hard into Pete's arms. The force toppled the boy backward and he landed on the coil of rope alongside the dock. With quick thinking, however, Pete kept the *Flying Cloud* from being damaged by holding it high.

Joey's rude actions, especially since he had promised to behave, angered Pete. Quickly handing the model to Dave, Pete sprang up and said, "Get out of our yard, Joey Brill!"

"Make me."

Pete gave the bully a shove. Joey pushed Pete. Instantly the boys were locked in a scuffle and the rope quickly became entangled about their legs.

By accident the rope looped around Joey's ankles and he toppled over. *Thump.* Joey's forehead hit the side of the boat hard. "Ow!" he yowled.

Pete helped him to his feet, saying he was sorry Joey had hit his head.

"It's all your fault!" Joey cried, dancing around in pain.

The noise brought Mrs. Hollister from the house with Pam and Holly to see what had happened. A large red lump had begun to rise over Joey's right eye.

Mrs. Hollister ran up to look at it. "Oh dear," she said, "I'm afraid you're going to have a black eye unless we do something fast. Perhaps we can get the swelling down with some ice." She sent Pam racing to the refrigerator for several cubes.

In a moment Pam returned with a dishful of ice. Her mother wrapped three in her handkerchief and pressed it against Joey's forehead.

"If you'll hold it there for several minutes, Joey, I'm sure the swelling will go down."

Mrs. Hollister advised him to go home and lie down until he felt better. "Keep putting fresh ice on your head," she advised.

Joey straddled his bike, still holding the ice to his forehead. Mrs. Hollister returned to the house and did not notice Joey again. He started to pedal up the path. Pete followed, carrying the ship model. Behind him was Holly.

She was the only one who kept her eye on the bully. As he reached the driveway, he suddenly

"You'd think your old boat was made of gold."

dismounted from his bicycle and drew back the hand holding the ice cubes.

"Look out, Pete!" Holly cried as Joey flung them toward her brother.

But Joey's aim was bad. *Crash!* The handkerchief full of ice sailed through the dining-room window! Glass shattered in all directions.

"Joey, you bad, bad boy!" Holly cried.

"It was an accident. Serves you right anyhow." Joey hopped on his bike and raced off just as Mrs. Hollister ran from the house.

"Joey did it!" Holly said.

Mrs. Hollister shook her head and said, "Something should be done about that boy."

"I'll put a new pane in tomorrow," Pete offered.

All the children worked on the clipper ship until suppertime. By then it began to look like a sleek sailing craft of the olden days. The sails billowed in the light breeze and Pete had to furl them in order to hold the rowboat at the dock.

"I can hardly wait till she's finished so I can take a ride in her," the boy said happily.

"She should be ready tomorrow," Pam answered.

That evening while the Hollisters were eating dessert of apple pie, a car drove up in front of their house.

"I'll guess it's Joey's father come to pay for the broken window," Mr. Hollister ventured.

"That would surprise me," Ricky said doubtfully. "I'll bet Joey never told his father."

Pete, who had risen from the table to greet the caller, looked through the screen door and exclaimed, "Wow!"

The children hopped up from the table to look. "I recognize that checkered jacket!" Pam cried. "That's the man who nearly ran into us."

The man, who wore no hat, had sandy blond hair which was thin and slicked down tight against his head.

"I'm Mr. Barrow of Pacific Coast Pictures," he introduced himself. "Is your father in?"

"Yes." Pete opened the door and asked Mr. Barrow to come into the living room. When all the Hollisters had been introduced to him by Pete, Mrs. Hollister said, "You're in the movie business?"

"Yes, I am," he replied. "Just came from California."

At this Pete and Pam glanced at each other. This certainly appeared to be the man who had nearly run over them.

"I was sent here by a friend of yours," Mr. Barrow went on.

"Yes?" Mr. Hollister said. "Who is it?"

"Tom King," came the startling reply.

The Hollisters were even more surprised when Mr. Barrow continued, "He sent me to pick up the copies of the clipper ship sketches."

91

CHAPTER 10

A MIXED-UP MYSTERY

ONE thought occurred to each of the Hollisters immediately: *Tom King had never mentioned knowing a Mr. Barrow.*

As far as they knew, the Hawaiian had no acquaintances in this country other than themselves.

Mr. Hollister, however, said cordially, "Please have a seat, sir, and we can talk this over."

Pete and Pam kept their eyes glued on the caller. They figured he was probably the same man who had followed them and had asked about Tom King at *The Trading Post.* Now he wanted the photostats. The children wondered why.

Mr. Barrow shifted his weight restlessly. "There's really nothing to talk over," he told Mr. Hollister. "And unfortunately I'm in a terrific hurry. So if you will give me the sketches . . ." His voice trailed off persuasively.

"I'm afraid we can't just hand them over to you," Mrs. Hollister said pleasantly. "You see, Mr. King entrusted them to our care."

"We have to keep them until he gets in touch with us," Holly piped up.

"And we don't know who you are," Mr.

Hollister said. "Have you anything by which to identify yourself, Mr. Barrow?"

"Of course, that's no problem," the man replied suavely, reaching for his wallet. He pulled it from his pocket and produced a letter, which he gave to Mr. Hollister.

The children crowded around him to see what it was. The letter was typed on Pacific Coast Motion Picture Company stationery, and identified Mr. Barrow as their eastern representative.

After reading it, Mr. Hollister handed it to his wife. "This looks all right to me," he said.

Mr. Barrow nodded. "I was sure there would be no question."

"Have you a letter from Tom King authorizing me to give you the photostats?" Mr. Hollister inquired.

Pam's heart leaped. At first she had been afraid her father might turn over the sketches. Now she realized that he, too, was a little suspicious of Mr. Barrow.

Their caller's eyes narrowed, but his voice remained calm as he said, "I'm afraid Tom did not consider that necessary."

Ricky could keep still no longer. "What do you want to do with the clipper ship pictures?" he asked.

Mr. Barrow's eyebrows lifted. "I don't wish to be rude, but frankly I can't see why that is any of your business, young man."

"But how do we know you're a friend of Tom's?" Pam asked. "We haven't heard about you!"

The caller's face grew red, but he struggled to control himself.

"Really, children, the prints of the old clipper ship have nothing to do with you!"

"But we found the brief case when it was lost," Ricky said. "Didn't Tom tell you about that?"

"Why, er—yes, he did," Barrow remarked, trying to manage a smile and regain his composure.

A plan to test the man's honesty occurred to Pete, and he said, "Did Tom tell you how we found his brief case in the auto repair garage?"

"Yes, indeed. I heard all about it," Barrow said, almost jovial again.

Pete wanted to blurt out that this was a lie, but he said nothing, merely glancing at his father with a significant look.

In a firm voice Mr. Hollister said, "I can't give you the photostats, Mr. Barrow, until you get a letter from Tom King asking me to do so."

"But—but I must have them now!" the man spluttered. "I demand that you hand them over!"

"Don't you do it, Dad!" Pete burst out. "I don't think he's telling the truth."

"Keep out of this!" Barrow exclaimed angrily.

Mr. Hollister gave the caller a piercing look.

"I think my children are right," he said, and

94

added, "If that's all you have to say now, please go."

"Not until I get——" the stranger started to say when Zip, hearing the loud voices, bounded from the kitchen.

The dog immediately sensed that something was wrong. When the caller glared at him, Zip uttered a low growl.

"Quiet, boy!" Pete commanded.

"Don't you dare turn your dog on me!" Barrow cried, backing toward the door.

"We're not," Pam said calmly.

"Keep him away!" Barrow cried as Zip continued his growling. The man reached for the knob, still eying Zip. Then, opening the door, he stepped outside. In a low menacing voice, he added, "You'll regret this!"

As Barrow drove away, Mrs. Hollister gave a big sigh. "This certainly is a mixed-up mystery, but I'm sure we did the right thing. If Tom King had wanted us to give his sketches to Barrow, he would have let us know."

The Hollisters were still talking about their strange visitor when a police car pulled into the driveway.

"Oh-oh!" Ricky said. "I'll bet Mr. Barrow made up some story about us to the police."

"He certainly has nothing to complain about!" Pete said angrily.

When a young man stepped from the car,

Holly cried, "It's Officer Cal!" She skipped onto the porch and raced across the lawn to meet their policeman friend.

"Did Mr. Barrow say anything bad about us?" Holly asked, tugging at the officer's hand.

"Barrow? I don't know anybody named Barrow," Cal said seriously. "That isn't what I came to see you about."

As the rest of the Hollisters hurried to meet him, Cal looked at them hesitantly for a moment, a worried expression on his face.

"You look awful glum," said Holly. "What's wrong?"

"I'm afraid I have bad news for you," the policeman replied.

"Has something happened to Domingo at Cousin Teddy's?" Ricky asked quickly.

"No, it's not that. Your friend Tom King has had back luck."

The Hollisters gasped and Sue whimpered, "Oh, I hope he's not hurt-ed!"

"Not seriously, anyhow," Cal said sympathetically. He told the Hollisters that the Massachusetts police had relayed a report to the Shoreham station that Tom King's car had been forced off the road by another auto. The two men in it had bound and gagged him.

"Why would they do a mean thing like that?" Ricky cried angrily.

"You'll regret this!"

"To rob him," Cal said tersely. "They stole the original sketches of the clipper ship!"

"How awful!" Pam cried.

"Is Tom all right now?" Mrs. Hollister asked in concern.

Cal said that although the Hawaiian had been roughed up a bit he was not hurt. "He went on to Orient Harbor," Cal added, "but without the sketches."

"There are three people after those drawings!" Pete exclaimed. He told the policeman about their mysterious caller, and wondered aloud if Barrow was in league with Tom's attackers.

"We think Barrow is a phony," Ricky explained.

"Would you check on him for us?" Pam pleaded.

"I can do that right away," Officer Cal said.

He went to his prowl car, with the Hollisters trailing behind him. Picking up his radio transmitter, he called headquarters, asking that a teletype be sent to California to check on the Pacific Coast Company and its agent, Mr. Barrow.

While waiting for a reply, the Hollisters discussed the mystery with Officer Cal. Why would anyone want the original sketches so badly that he would attack Tom? Also, why was Barrow's movie company so eager to get hold of the copies? And why had Mr. Dooley felt he should warn them to guard the photostats?

"You Hollisters have landed in the middle of

another big riddle," Cal said, smiling. "I hope you'll be able to solve this case as well as you have the others you tackled."

Just then Cal was called to the radio and a hollow-sounding voice at headquarters said, "There is no such movie company on the West Coast."

"He was a fake!" Pam cried.

"Our Zip knew he was a bad man right away," Holly said proudly, patting their dog.

Quickly the children gave Cal a description of the man and also of his car. "I'll be on the lookout for him," he promised.

"Maybe you had better take the sketches and put them in the police department safe for us," said Pete.

"I'll be glad to," the officer replied.

Pam went for the photostats and gave them to the policeman. Then, with a wave to him, they watched him back his car out of the driveway and ride off.

All the youngsters were so excited about the mystery that they were unable to settle down when bedtime came. Ricky, putting on his pajamas, heard Sue and Holly giggling in the next room. The boy knocked and peeked in.

"Let's play a game!" he said.

"What?" Holly asked.

"How about *jumping on the balloon?*"

Ricky's suggestion was met by whoops of delight from his sisters. The boy had invented the game some time before. It consisted of lifting one end of the bed sheet and pulling it down rapidly, trapping air inside. This looked like the top of a balloon. Then the children would stand at the foot of the bed and jump onto the billowy cloth.

"Your turn first, Sue," Holly said as she puffed the sheet.

The little girl jumped. *Plop!* The sheet flattened out and Sue squealed with delight.

"Whoopee!" she cried.

When it was Holly's turn, she landed so hard that she bounded back a foot into the air!

"Okay. Now let me try," Ricky begged.

Holly puffed the sheet extra-high as Ricky perched on the foot of the bed. "Here I go!" he called.

But instead of landing in the center of the "balloon," Ricky skidded off to one side and landed *thump* on the floor.

"Goodness, what was that?" Mrs. Hollister cried, running upstairs in fright. "Who fell?"

"Me." Ricky grinned sheepishly as he got off the floor, rubbing his right thigh. He put on an exaggerated limp and made a wry face to make his sisters laugh. Then he disappeared into his own room, saying he was all right.

When Sue said her prayers she included one for Tom King, asking that he be kept safe and recover his stolen property.

"I just know everything will be all right," she said, getting off her knees and climbing into bed as Holly rose too and went to her room.

Zip sprang onto Sue's bed and lay at her feet. Soon the whole house was quiet, with everybody asleep. In the middle of the night Zip stirred and his ears pricked up. Then, with a whine and a short bark, he jumped to the floor.

The movement awakened Sue immediately. "Zip, what's wrong?" she asked, but the dog was already on his way to the first floor. The little girl heard him give a sharp bark.

Frightened, Sue hopped out of bed and went to awaken Pam in the next room. "Hurry," she said. "Something's the matter downstairs."

Pam sat upright and listened. Zip's barks turned into a low whine and then ceased entirely.

By this time the whole family had been aroused. Slipping on their robes, they flicked on the lights and went downstairs to find out what was wrong.

Pete glanced toward the desk in the corner of the living room. The top drawer was open, and papers lay scattered on the floor!

Pam was the first to see Zip lying near the desk. Uttering a cry, she raced over to him.

The lovely collie was unconscious!

CHAPTER 11

RESCUED!

For a second the Hollisters stood in stunned silence, then Pam cried out, "Zip! What happened to you?"

She hurried for a cup of cool water. Pete dipped his fingers into it and sprinkled the dog's muzzle. Soon Zip began to stir, and Pam and the others sighed with relief.

Meanwhile Ricky and Mr. Hollister were examining the desk drawer, shuffling through the papers. "Someone broke into our house!" the boy cried.

"He was trying to get the photostats!" Holly declared.

"You're right," her father agreed. "Good thing Cal took them to headquarters." He turned to Pete and Pam. "How's Zip?"

By now their pet was on his feet. He acted a little groggy but seemed all right otherwise.

"What happened, old boy?" Pete asked him.

The dog barked and walked across the floor to the dining room, stopping at the broken window.

"This is how the intruder got in and escaped, too," Pete said.

"But how did he knock Zip out?" Ricky pondered.

Pam examined her pet thoroughly but could find no mark or telltale bruise.

"He could have used chloroform in a handkerchief or a wad of cotton," Mr. Hollister suggested. "In fact, I think there's still a faint odor of chloroform in the room."

The others sniffed and nodded, thinking how important the sketches must be to someone—or perhaps several people—besides Tom King. But why?

After making sure their pet had recovered, the Hollisters debated whether or not to telephone the police immediately. But since nothing of value had been taken, they decided to wait until morning.

Immediately after an early breakfast next day, Mr. Hollister called headquarters. Within twenty minutes Officer Cal arrived with fingerprint equipment and examined the various prints on the desk drawer. All of them belonged to the Hollisters.

"I guess one of you must be the burglar," the young policeman joked. Then he added seriously, "The fellow who broke in evidently wore gloves."

"Then we have no clues about who he was," Pam remarked with a sigh.

"I wouldn't say that," Cal replied. "I'm sure that Barrow was the man."

The Hollisters were startled. "Then you must have found out something more about him," the children's father said.

Officer Cal nodded. He explained that during the night the police had uncovered a great deal of information concerning the man. First of all, his car was found abandoned on a road outside Shoreham.

"It had been stolen in California," the officer added grimly. "We got a report on that."

He told how a check on Barrow's record had revealed that he was a well-known confidence man who sometimes worked in the employ of others.

"I wonder how he learned about the photostats in the first place?" Pam mused. "Do you think Joey Brill might have had something to do with it? He knew about the sketches."

"It wouldn't hurt to ask him," Pete said. "If Mr. Barrow saw him here and questioned him, Joey would probably have mentioned the sketches."

Officer Cal offered to drive the two older children to Joey's house. When they arrived, the bully himself answered the door. His eye was as purple as a winter turnip!

"We'd like to ask you a few questions," Officer Cal said.

"Oh dear, a policeman! Is something wrong?" Mrs. Brill cried, hurrying in to see who the callers were.

Officer Cal assured her it was nothing to worry about and explained that he was looking for clues concerning the Hollister housebreaking. Both Joey and his mother were startled to hear about it.

"That's too bad," said Mrs. Brill. "And I'm glad the intruder didn't injure your dog permanently."

"Do you know a man named Barrow?" the policeman asked Joey.

At first the boy did not want to reply, but his mother prodded him. "It's your duty to tell the officer what you know," she insisted.

"All right," Joey said sullenly. "I know him. I met Mr. Barrow just after I broke your window yesterday."

The boy explained that Mr. Barrow had been parked near the Hollister home. When Joey passed him on his bicycle, the man had stopped him.

"What did he ask you?" Cal said.

"If I knew anything about the Hollisters."

"Something in particular?" Pam questioned.

Joey nodded. "He wanted to know if you had copies of some clipper ship sketches."

"Did you tell him we did?" Pete asked.

"Sure. Why not?" Joey countered.

"That explains it," Pete said, striking his palm with his fist. "After Mr. Barrow couldn't talk us into giving him the sketches, he broke into our house last night to steal them!"

Pete explained that Officer Cal had taken the photostats to headquarters earlier in the evening.

Mrs. Brill seemed relieved that the prints had not been stolen, so her son was not involved. She said she was sure Joey did not realize he might cause trouble for the Hollisters by talking to the man.

"Yeah . . ." Joey muttered unconvincingly.

"However," she added, "I did *not* know Joey had broken your window!" Speaking sternly to her son, she ordered him to buy a new pane of glass and replace the broken window himself.

Joey promised that he would do this and asked Pete to give him the proper dimensions. Then Cal drove the Hollisters home. Pete made the measurements and phoned them to Joey.

After lunch Joey came to the Hollisters' home with a new piece of window glass, a can of putty, and a box of glazier's points. Without a word to anyone, he replaced the broken pane and went home.

Ricky, upon seeing it, grinned. "For once that guy came across," he murmured.

Meanwhile the Hollister children continued their work on the rowboat clipper.

"I think she's ready for a trial run now," Pete said as he untied the boat from the dock about four o'clock.

With all the clipper ship gear rigged, there was not much room in the boat itself, so Pete decided to take only Ricky along for a sail. His brother sat down in the bow while Pete got in the stern to operate an oar for steering.

It was a beautiful cloudless day. A good breeze blew across Pine Lake toward the state park at the upper end.

At first the boys had trouble getting the sails to fill because the wind was tricky and puffy off the land. First they would flap, then fill suddenly, making the boat surge ahead swiftly.

A little way offshore a good puff suddenly hit the sails. The boat shot out toward the middle of the lake.

"Yikes!" Ricky shouted with a grin. "Look at us go!"

"We'll be around Cape Horn in no time," cried Pete, trying to make his voice sound like an old-time sea captain's.

The boat made a startling picture as it sped along, and people in motorboats and fishing craft gazed in amazement and admiration. The boys waved gaily and Ricky struck a pose, shading his eyes and pretending to be a lookout.

"Ship ahoy!" he shouted.

As they sailed farther out, the wind became stronger. Free of the land, it kicked up whitecaps that rolled along in the boat's wake. Pete had to use all his strength to hold the steering oar straight.

"Getting kind of rough out here in the trade wind belt," he said, carrying on his game of talking like an old salt. "Guess we'd better change course for land."

"Aye, aye, sir," Ricky answered, saluting and returning to his lookout pose.

Pete pushed the oar over to change course, shoving hard against the pressure of the water. The boat answered slowly until the wind was coming across the side a bit.

All of a sudden, as the bow turned more, several of the sails caught the wind on the other side and the boat began to tip.

"Whoa!" Pete yelled in surprise.

He and Ricky jumped to the high side to keep their ship from tipping more. It started to go over farther, but the pressure on the oar was too much for Pete and he had to let it come out of the water. It was just in time, too. The boat straightened up, but not before some water splashed over the gunwale.

Suddenly from the top of the mainmast came a sound of ripping cloth as the skysail tore and began to flap wildly in the breeze.

"What's the matter, Pete?" Ricky asked worriedly.

"Crickets, I don't know! She won't go where I want her to," Pete said.

The boat began to tip.

With the oar out of the water, the boat steered herself back on the old course, with the wind directly over the stern. They were far out in the lake now, still headed for the park.

"How will we get back?" Ricky asked, worried.

For answer, Pete tried to turn the boat again, but the same thing happened. "She only goes one way!" he exclaimed. "We'll just have to land on the other shore."

The boat sped on across the lake faster and faster, and Pete began to scan the shore ahead anxiously. They were being swept into a cove near the state park. This inlet was marked by two rocky points and its shore was a tumble of boulders, upon which the wind-whipped waves splashed wildly. Halfway up the cove was a low automobile bridge on heavy pilings.

"Crickets!" Pete muttered. "This is no place to land." He tried with all his strength to steer the boat toward more protected water, but the wind had it in charge now and was sweeping it directly toward the bridge!

Pete lifted the oar into the boat and got out his pocket knife. "I'm going to cut down the sails," he called to Ricky. "Lend a hand."

Whipping out his own knife, Ricky jumped to help his brother. Quickly they cut through the rigging which they had worked so hard to put up, and one by one the sails tumbled into the boat.

Despite this, the boat continued to drift rapidly

and now was dangerously close to the bridge. The waves were surging and splashing under it and the pilings gleamed black and ugly.

Ricky crawled back to his post in the prow. "We're going to hit, Pete!" Ricky tried to keep the fear out of his voice. "What'll we do?"

"I'll try to hold us off so you can climb up," Pete said. "Sit still and keep your hands inside the boat till I tell you what to do."

"Okay," Ricky said in a small voice. Suddenly his eyes brightened. "Pete, here comes Dave's motorboat!"

Bouncing at top speed over the waves, their friend's boat headed toward them. Dave was crouched over the motor, peering ahead, and a bearded young man sat in the forward seat urging him on.

The little outboard skiff came up to them quickly, and Dave threw a coil of rope over toward Ricky. But in his excitement he threw too soon and it fell short in the water. Ricky tried to reach the line, almost tumbling in, but his arms were too short. The brothers watched in despair as the rope was sucked into the propeller and Dave's motor stopped with a shudder.

Now the bearded man moved swiftly. Seizing a paddle, he brought Dave's boat alongside the foundering rowboat clipper ship and leaped on board, fastening the bowline of Dave's boat around a seat.

In a strong, clear voice, he began to give orders. "Get that line clear as fast as you can," he told Dave, handing the paddle to Pete as he spoke.

He picked up the steering oar and began to use it as a paddle with great, strong strokes.

"Paddle for all you're worth," he encouraged Pete. "We'll hold her here till that line is cleared."

Seeing Ricky's worried face, he grinned broadly. "Hi, redhead! How about grabbing one of those loose floor boards and paddling too?"

Ricky picked up the board and was soon paddling manfully. With the three of them working hard, the clipper ship was almost holding its own against the waves. But she was within a few feet of the menacing pilings!

After several moments of paddling, Pete thought his aching arms would drop off. He did not see how he could paddle much longer!

But just in time he heard Dave shout, "She's free!"

Dave quickly pulled the starting rope and his engine coughed into action. Putting it in reverse, he backed the boats away from the menacing black pilings until they were far enough out to rig the towline properly.

With the clipper ship safely in tow and Pete and Ricky sitting next to the bearded stranger, they started back across the lake for the dock.

Pete smiled at the man in gratitude. "You sure

saved us just in time!" he said. "Thanks! But why wouldn't the boat steer?"

"You made a beautiful clipper ship," the man said, "but I'm afraid you forgot one thing. Without a keel underneath and without extra sails like jibs and spankers, a clipper ship will only go before the wind."

Ricky looked at Pete and grinned. "We goofed!" he said. The bearded man threw back his head, roaring with laughter.

Soon the rowboat clipper was secure at the side of the Hollisters' dock, and the bearded man stepped ashore. He explained that he had been walking along the lake front looking for the Hollister home and had asked Dave for directions. Just then they had seen the sailboat in distress and had gone to its aid.

During the explanation Pete had been studying their tall rescuer with curiosity. Somehow his face looked very familiar. Where had he seen him before?

Ricky, too, was puzzled by a faint sense of recognition. Who could the man be?

Suddenly the stranger noticed their stares and grinned. "What's the matter, boys? Never seen a beard before?"

"That voice!" Pete thought as Pam, Sue, and Holly rushed up to the group on the dock. He recognized the stranger's voice now and cried, "You're Gregory Grant, the movie actor!"

CHAPTER 12

FAMOUS VISITORS

PAM could hardly believe that this was Gregory Grant, the movie star. "You're—you're really here right on our own dock!" she cried.

The momentary surprise on the faces of all the children turned to looks of delight. Each one of them grinned and shook hands with the actor.

"Pinch me," Holly said. "I can't believe it." The man chuckled, his dark eyes dancing.

By now Pam had recovered sufficiently to say, "You came to see us, Mr. Grant?"

"Just call me Greg," he replied, smiling. "And my reason for being here is quite a story. I'll tell you about it later. But first I'd like you to meet my wife."

He walked toward the house and down the driveway, where a light-colored sports car was parked at the curb. The children followed him as far as the front yard.

Dave Mead gave a long whistle and exclaimed, "Gregory Grant! Wait'll the other kids hear this!"

"I just can't wait to learn why he came to see us," Pam said, her face flushed with excitement.

A few moments later the actor helped a young woman from the car and escorted her to the children. She was beautiful and walked gracefully. A scarf was thrown over her blond hair and she wore dark glasses.

At once the children recognized her as Lisa Sarno. They smiled in greeting.

Then Ricky burst out, "Have you come to make a movie in Shoreham?"

And Pam added, "Only the other day I was making believe I was you in a home movie we were doing."

Lisa Sarno laughed gaily as they all entered the house. "What a charming home you have!" she said as she walked into the living room.

"Thank you," said Pam, then introduced her mother.

Mrs. Hollister was as surprised as her children had been to meet the famous couple. After seating themselves in comfortable chairs, the actor and actress explained why they had come to Shoreham. Their next picture, they said, was to be called *The Clue of the Clipper Ship*, and was to be filmed at Orient Harbor, Massachusetts.

"Lisa and I thought we would drive in a leisurely way from the West as a little vacation before starting work," Greg added.

He explained that every night they made a telephone call to their director, who already had arrived at Orient Harbor.

"And when we called last night," Lisa said,

"we were told that a man named Tom King had arrived with some very valuable information."

"You mean he found the sketches of the clipper ship that were stolen from him?" Pete broke in, and explained the theft, about which, it turned out, Mr. Grant already knew.

Greg said that he was sorry to say no to Pete's question. "But," he added, "King identified his ship pictures as being of the *Winged Chief*."

"How did he do that?" Pam asked.

"From an old clipper model at the museum," Greg replied. "They were identical."

"And that's why we're visiting you," Lisa put in. "Mr. King said that you have a copy of his drawings. Our motion picture company would like to have them to use in designing some of the sets. So we'll take them."

The Hollisters looked at one another. Was this a new trick to get the valuable drawings?

"But these really are movie stars," Pam told herself. "Besides, how could such nice, well-known people be dishonest?"

Before anyone had a chance to say yes or no to the proposal, they all heard a motor scooter from the post office chugging down the street. It stopped at the Hollister home. A young man wearing a peaked cap got off and strode up the walk.

"Will somebody sign for a registered letter?" he asked Pam, who had gone to the door.

"I will," she said.

Pam signed the receipt and the postman gave her a letter. Suddenly he saw the actor and his wife in the living room. His mouth fell open.

"Wow!" he said. "Pardon me, but are these folks friends of yours?"

The Hollister children, looking into the hall, smiled and nodded their heads proudly. The postman made a bow, then asked, "May I shake hands with them?"

"Of course," Greg grinned, rising and walking into the hall. "I'm glad to meet you, Mr. ——"

"Homer—Homer Wakefield," stammered the youth.

Lisa joined her husband and they both shook hands with Homer.

"Wait till the boys at the special-delivery window hear this!" he exclaimed. Homer raced to the curb, hopped on his motor scooter, and putted off.

As the rest of the Hollisters chuckled, Pam glanced at the return address on the registered letter. Her eyes sparkled as she said, "It's from Tom King!"

Everyone was quiet as she read it aloud. Tom had started the letter by saying that he had had a lovely time visiting the Hollisters and appreciated all the nice things they had done for him. Then he said:

"You probably have heard by now that my

sketches were stolen. But with Mr. Dooley's help I identified my grandfather's ship as the *Winged Chief*. A movie company would like a copy of the sketches and I am told that Gregory Grant and Lisa Sarno will stop off at your house to pick them up. You have my permission to give them the prints.

"I hope that I may see you all soon again. Give my best to everybody, including my pal Zip."

It was signed "Tom King."

The Hollisters, besides being glad to hear from Tom, were relieved to know that their visitors were entitled to take the pictures.

"At present they're at the police station for safekeeping," Mrs. Hollister told the couple, and gave the reason.

Lisa and Gregory were shocked to hear that an attempt had been made to steal them from the Hollister home. "It looks as if our moving pictures aren't any more exciting than things that go on here in Shoreham," Lisa said, smiling.

Mrs. Hollister told the actors it would take a little time to get the photostats, so she cordially invited the couple to stay and have supper with the family. They readily accepted, and Pete said:

"I'll hop down to the headquarters on my bicycle and pick up the prints."

"And I'll go with you," Pam said. "You'll need

help if anyone stops you and tries to take the sketches."

The children pedaled out of the driveway and headed for police headquarters. They had gone only a short distance when a girl named Carol, who was in Pam's class, dashed into the street, waving her arms.

"Is it true?" she asked. "Are movie stars at your house?"

Pam said it was true, and Carol sighed, "How I'd love to meet them!" Pam offered to see if this could be arranged, then excused herself and set off once more.

But the same question was asked again and again as she and Pete hurried along. Children would dash up and stop them, asking, "Are Gregory Grant and Lisa Sarno really at your home?"

"It's amazing how news spreads," Pam remarked as she and her brother neared the center of town.

Hopping off their bikes, they ran up the steps of the police station and hurried to the room where Officer Cal could often be found. As the two entered, they discovered the policeman seated at a desk, making out a report. When he saw them he said with a grin:

"Don't tell me—you have movie stars at your home. What next will you Hollisters be doing!"

The children laughed and quickly told Cal the whole story. "And now we would like the

119

photostats," Pam added, "because Lisa and Gregory want to take them to Orient Harbor."

Cal picked up a telephone and called the chief, in whose safe the pictures were stored. In a few moments another policeman walked in with them.

"Thanks so much," Pete said.

"Don't lose the sketches," Cal advised. Then he smiled and added, "I have an idea. How would you two like a police escort back to your house?"

Pam and Pete were speechless for a moment. Then Pete said, "You mean a patrol-car escort for our bicycles?"

"Sure. Why not? You have valuable property to carry."

"Let's go!"

Cal arose from the desk, put on his policeman's cap, and started out a rear door. "I'll meet you in front of the building."

He selected the prowl car which he usually used and drove out of the parking area. Pausing a moment, he called to the Hollisters, "Follow me!"

Pete carried the sketches and Pam rode alongside him. They stayed about ten feet behind the police car, which sounded its siren softly as it snaked down one street and up another.

Once on Shoreham Road, Cal went a little faster and the Hollisters pedaled gleefully behind him. Groups of children they passed along the way turned to stare at the strange sight. Never before had they seen a policeman clear the way for two cyclists!

When they came to the Hollister home, Cal waved good-by and the children raced into their driveway. "We're here!" Pete shouted, entering the living room. "We have the sketches!"

Gregory was playing hide-and-seek with Sue and did not reply. Lisa, who was chatting with Ricky and Holly about famous make-up artists on the movie sets, smiled and said, "That's fine."

What fun everyone had at supper! The movie stars were natural, charming people and were completely at ease with the Hollister family. The children talked about the latest Western movie they had seen, in which Gregory was the hero and Lisa the kidnaped daughter of a poor rancher.

"Was it really you who tumbled over the cliff, Greg?" Ricky wanted to know.

"I'm afraid not," the actor replied frankly. "That was a dummy."

"Aw," said Ricky, disappointed. "But how about the man who jumped off the horse to grab the outlaw?"

When Gregory said that he had played that scene, Ricky seemed pleased and relieved. "Will you make some movies for us tonight?" he asked eagerly.

Gregory and Lisa were startled at this proposal. "But we have no director," Lisa said.

"I'll tell you what to do," Ricky piped up.

The actor bucked up and down like a bronco.

His remark caused much merriment, and the stars gaily agreed to follow the boy's commands and make a picture.

After dinner Pete brought his movie equipment down from the attic and set it up in the living room. Tinker had sent out new lights from *The Trading Post*, so everything was in order.

"We must have a real dramatic scene," Lisa said, getting into the spirit of the fun. "What shall it be?"

Sue was ready with an answer. "I'd like Greg to be my horse and I'll be the cowgirl."

The actor laughed so hard that he could hardly get down on his hands and knees. Then, with Sue on his back, he bucked up and down like a bronco while Pete operated the movie camera.

The rest of the film was of scenes showing the stars chatting with the Hollisters in their living room and singing songs around the piano.

Then, as Pete put his equipment away, Lisa said, "And now I have a surprise for you Hollisters."

"Goody, goody! What is it?" Sue said, jumping up and down.

All the children listened intently as the actress continued, "How would you like to come to Orient Harbor and act as extras in our clipper ship pictures?"

CHAPTER 13

GOOD-BY TO PIGTAILS

LISA SARNO chuckled over the looks of amazement on the faces of the Hollister children. "You will act in our picture, won't you?" she asked.

"Will we!" Ricky shouted.

"How perfectly wonderful!" Pam declared as all the children began to voice their delight at once.

"But they've never had any acting experience." Mrs. Hollister spoke up. "Could you really use them as extras?"

"Of course we could," Greg put in. "I think all your children are natural-born performers. We'll find a good place for them in our movie."

"You're very kind," Mrs. Hollister told the movie stars, "but our family had a vacation a short while ago, and we must consider the expense."

"Aw, we wouldn't eat much!" Ricky said with a pleading look.

Mr. Hollister smiled at his family. "I think such a trip might be arranged," he said. "And I think it would be good for the children's education to see part of Massachusetts."

"Don't worry about the expenses," added Greg quickly. "Grand-American Pictures, which is producing the film, will take care of your expenses and pay the little actors a salary in addition."

Pete and Pam beamed with delight as Ricky, Holly, and Sue pranced about joyfully.

"I'm an actor!" Ricky cried, hooking his thumbs under his arms and strutting about. "Heap big chief!"

"You're not an actor yet!" Pam warned. "Not until after you've passed your screen test."

"And you might flunk it," Holly giggled.

But their words did not deflate Ricky, who instantly stood on his head to show Lisa and Greg how versatile he was. They laughed and clapped.

"I'd like to make the trip too," Mr. Hollister said. "But I'm afraid I shall have to stay in Shoreham to take care of my business."

It was decided that they would take the train to Orient Harbor in two days. "That will give us time to pack," Mrs. Hollister said.

The movie stars were plied with a dozen questions by the eager Hollister children. One came from Pam. "Will we have to use make-up?"

"Of course," Lisa replied. Then she cocked her head, saying, "You know, Pam, I believe I could make you up to look exactly like me."

"Do it, then," Ricky said. "I'd like to see my sister look like a real actress."

Lisa winked at Greg and said, "Will you bring in the kit, dear?"

Greg arose and went to his car, returning in a

few moments with a small suitcase. Lisa opened it. Inside was a complete array of make-up equipment in attractive jars, bottles, and boxes.

Pete hurried off for a kitchen stool. Pam sat primly upon it while Lisa went about her work with skillful hands. First she applied a special cream on Pam's face which covered up the Hollister girl's few freckles. Then she deftly put on eyebrow pencil and mascara.

Pam blinked her eyes in what she thought was a starry expression. Pete gave a low whistle. "You look dreamy, Sis!"

"Real gruesome!" kidded Ricky.

"Oh, she's not finished yet," Lisa said, smiling. After she had dusted a light powder over Pam's face, she unscrewed a fresh red lipstick. Holding Pam's chin with her left hand, she accentuated the girl's pretty mouth with the rouge.

"One thing more," the movie star said, and she combed Pam's hair in a sleek style much like her own.

"Now," she said as Pam stood up, "go to the mirror and see yourself."

Pam hurried over to look in the mirror over the fireplace. "Oh!" she gasped. "I hardly recognize myself. Will I look like this when I'm older?"

"If you do," chuckled Lisa, "I may be out of a job!"

Mr. and Mrs. Hollister, too, agreed that their daughter looked very much like Lisa Sarno. As the actress began to put things back into her make-up kit, she suddenly gazed around with a perplexed expression.

"What is it, Lisa?" Mrs. Hollister asked.

"My other lipstick. It was right here a minute ago."

Pam now noticed that Sue was no longer in the room. Had she taken it? Pam called to her little sister.

"Here I am!" Sue replied. "Upstairs in my room."

"What are you doing, honey?" called her mother.

No reply came from the little girl. Instead her footsteps could be heard coming down the stairs, and she burst into the living room giggling.

"Am I as pretty as Pam?" she asked.

"Good gracious!" Mrs. Hollister exclaimed, and everyone burst out laughing. Sue had applied lipstick to her own little pink mouth, making it appear twice its normal size.

"I love lickstick," Sue said, grinning, " 'cause it tastes like cotton candy." Then she laughed. "Besides, I want to be a movie star, too."

She began moving her mouth into different shapes, making everyone laugh all the harder. Then she skipped gaily over to Lisa and handed her the lipstick.

"You do look different," Lisa said as she took

a tissue from the box and removed the smeary color.

"That's better," Mrs. Hollister said as she gave her daughter a hug. "But next time please ask before you borrow someone's possessions."

Shortly afterward Greg and Lisa said they must leave. After giving them the photostats of the clipper ship sketches, the Hollisters bade their new friends good-by.

"Don't forget, we'll see you soon," Lisa cried, waving as their car started off.

Pam was reluctant to take off her "movie face," as she called it. But before going to bed, she used cold cream to remove all her make-up.

Next day feverish excitement reigned in the Hollister home. Not only was everyone looking forward to the Orient Harbor visit and the movie, but also now the children might have a chance to help Tom King solve the mystery about his inheritance.

Each of the Hollisters kept a small suitcase in the attic. These were dusted and brought down. The children took clothes from their dressers and closets to pack.

Pete and Ricky finished their preparations in a jiffy and dashed out of the house long before the girls finished.

"Let's tell our friends about the trip," Ricky said.

Jumping on their bikes, the boys rode first to

Dave Mead's. "That's keen!" Dave said. "Will you send me a post card from Orient Harbor?"

"Sure, and maybe we can get Greg and Lisa to autograph it," Ricky said.

"Won't it be great when the movie comes to Shoreham?" Dave said. "Imagine seeing my pals on the screen!"

"Yes, but the big thing is to solve Tom King's mystery," Pete reminded his friend. Then he added, "Dave, why don't you sail our clipper ship while we're gone?"

Dave was pleased with this idea and promised to take good care of the converted rowboat.

The boys' next stop was at Jeff and Ann Hunter's. They too were delighted to hear of the Hollisters' good fortune. On the way home again the boys met Joey and Will, who were throwing stones at a squirrel in a tree.

"Shall we tell them?" Ricky whispered to his brother.

"Let's ride past them," Pete advised.

But before they could do this, Will called out, "You don't have to tell us. We know all about it!"

"Yeah," Joey said, "you've told everyone you're going to be actors. Pooh! I don't believe it!"

"We are, too," Ricky said hotly. "We're going to Orient Harbor to act with Greg and Lisa."

"That's what you think!" Will said slyly.

"What do you mean?" Pete asked.

"I'll bet you an old squirrel's tail," Joey taunted, "that you'll never get there."

Pete turned to his brother. "Come on, let's not argue with them."

The bullies were soon forgotten in the afternoon's activity. A shopping trip was made downtown, where Sue got a new sun suit, and Pam and Holly purchased shorts. Pete and Ricky bought new white polo shirts.

After supper Mrs. Hollister said, "I think we're finally ready for our trip to Orient Harbor."

"I've made train reservations for you in the sleeper," Mr. Hollister said, adding that he was lucky enough to get two bedrooms.

"That ought to be fun," Ricky said. He liked to ride on trains. On a trip to Canada he had become lost and his mother had found him helping the chef in the galley of the dining car.

Now, as Pete and Pam helped clear the supper dishes, Holly beckoned to Sue. "Come upstairs. I want to talk with you," she said.

The two girls ascended the steps to Holly's room. "How do you like my hair style, Sue?" Holly asked as she twirled her pigtails.

"It's nice," Sue said, looking at her sister. "Why?"

"Don't you think I'd look better with short hair?" Holly asked, pulling the braids into a bun. "Who ever heard of a movie actress wearing pigtails?"

The little girl, who thought that everything Holly said was just right, agreed with her. But she added, "How can you have short hair and pigtails at the same time?"

"I'll cut the pigtails off!"

"Oh! What will Mother say?"

Holly told her sister that Pam once had had pigtails but had cut them off. "Anyway, Mother cut off some and it didn't matter."

"Are you going to cut your own hair?" Sue asked.

"No, you are."

"Oh goody! I like to cut hair," the little girl said. She had not done this since she cut the bangs on her doll.

"I'll get the scissors," Holly offered.

She went into her mother's room and returned with a pair of large shears.

"I think you can snip off the braids," Holly instructed the younger girl. She kneeled on the floor and showed her sister exactly where she wanted the braids cut.

"Here?" Sue asked, opening the shears.

"No, a little shorter."

Just then Pam called from downstairs. "Holly, Sue, where are you? I'll read you a story before bedtime."

"Here we are," Sue called out.

"You're very quiet," her sister said. "What are you doing?"

"Shall I cut it here?" Sue asked.

"I'm going to cut Holly's hair off."

"What!"

Pam leaped up the stairs two at a time and burst into Holly's room. "Cut your pigtails? No!"

Pam took the scissors away from Sue just in time.

"But I have to look grown-up if I want to be an actress," Holly said, disappointed.

Mrs. Hollister came up to see what the fuss was about and was horrified to hear what had nearly taken place.

"But, Holly," she said, "if you're going to play the part of an old-fashioned girl in the movie you'll need your pigtails."

"Of course," Pam assured her. "Every girl wore them in clipper ship days."

Just as Holly was convinced that she should keep her lovely braids, the front door bell rang. Pete hurried to answer it. He was handed a telegram by a uniformed boy. After signing for it, Pete called the others. Ripping open the envelope, he said, "It's addressed to the Hollisters." Then he uttered a cry of astonishment.

"What's the matter?" his mother said, hurrying down with the girls.

"Listen to this," Pete said in a disappointed voice.

" 'No need to come to Orient Harbor. Extras already signed for the job.'

"Signed, 'Gregory.' "

CHAPTER 14

A FUNNY MISTAKE

HEARING the telegram, Holly burst into tears.

"I—I—want to be an actress!" she sobbed.

"So do I!" Sue cried, and little tears of sadness ran down the side of her nose.

Even Pam's eyes were moist, and Mrs. Hollister tried to console the children. "We all have disappointments," she said.

Pete, in reading the telegram again, suddenly shouted, "Hey, look at this!" He pointed out a line near the top of the telegram which read: SHOREHAM. Nowhere on the telegram did it mention Orient Harbor.

"Then it was sent from right here in town!" Pam said, drying her eyes.

"Sure!" Pete declared. "This is a hoax."

"You mean a big joke?" Holly asked.

"Yes." Pete narrowed his eyes and drew a deep breath. "I think I know who did this." He turned to Ricky. "Remember Joey told us we would never go to Orient Harbor? I think he sent the telegram."

"Then—then you mean we can be movie stars after all?" Sue stammered eagerly.

"Yes," Mrs. Hollister said, smiling.

Just to make certain he was right in his guess, Pete telephoned the local telegraph office and was assured that the message had been sent from town. But the man who had taken it was off duty.

"Drop in tomorrow and he'll tell you."

After breakfast next morning Pete drove downtown with his father, who dropped him at the telegraph office on his way to work. The clerk said that he had taken the telegram from two boys who had frankly admitted it was a prank.

"They said you'd get a laugh out of it," the man explained.

From a description of the lads Pete felt certain that they were Joey Brill and Will Wilson. "The joke is on them after all," he said, "because we're going to Orient Harbor and act in a movie." The clerk wished them luck.

That afternoon Pete sent Tom King a telegram informing him of their arrival time, then Mr. Hollister drove his family to the station. With Zip barking a final good-by, the children waved from the windows of their sleeper.

"Yikes, we're off to Orient Harbor!" Ricky shouted.

Soon Shoreham was disappearing from sight as the train sped toward the seashore. The Hollisters' spacious rooms were side by side, off a long corridor which ran down one side of the car. After the porter had stowed their baggage, the

children and their mother decided to have some
soda and cookies, so they walked back to the club
car, which was midway in the train. Here there
were restful seats and large picture windows.

Soon the Hollisters were enjoying their drinks
and watching the scenery as the train raced along.

"I think I'll write a note to Daddy," Pam said
presently.

She walked to the end of the car, where she
had noticed a built-in writing table and chair.
Selecting a post card which advertised the railroad
company, she jotted a note.

Picking up a small blotter, Pam noticed a series
of up-and-down letters which were backward. "It
looks like our name," she thought, mystified.

After dropping the post card into the train's
mailbox, Pam took the blotter and showed it to
her mother. "May I see the mirror in your purse?"
she asked.

Mrs. Hollister handed it to her daughter and
Pam tilted the glass against the blotter.

"It does say Hollister!" she whispered excitedly.
"Do you think someone was writing to us?"

"What do the other words say?" Mrs. Hollister
asked as the children listened intently.

Although the words were not plain, Pam studied
them carefully. Then she uttered a little cry and
read, " 'Plans ruined by Hollisters, but——' "

"Someone on this train is an enemy of ours!"
Pete declared.

His mother agreed that the blotted note seemed to indicate this. "But it may have been written yesterday or the day before," she said.

"But the person *could* be on the train right now," Pam remarked.

"Let's search it from end to end," Ricky suggested.

Mrs. Hollister gave the older children permission, saying she would stay in the club car with Sue. "Be very careful and don't make any foolish mistakes," she warned as they set off toward the front of the train.

Pete led the way, opening the doors for the others. The children passed from car to car, but there was no sign of Mr. Barrow. When they came to the front of the train, the conductor noticed them and said, "Are you looking for someone?"

"Yes, a man named Barrow," Pete said.

"There's no one holding reservations under that name," the conductor said. Then, smiling, he added, "I hope you find him."

The children hastened back to their mother. "Any luck?" she asked.

Pete shook his head. "Now we'll search the cars to the rear," he said, and they started off again.

The children lurched and swayed as they made their way along the corridor. Presently they came to the dining car. Pete opened the door and they stepped inside. Pam grabbed his arm. "Look at the other end of the car!"

The Hollisters stood still and gazed at a man seated with his back toward them. He wore a checkered jacket and his hair appeared to be thin and blond.

"That's Mr. Barrow all right," Ricky whispered.

"What'll we do?" Holly asked.

"I'll grab him," Pete said. "And if he tries to get away, the rest of you can hold on."

The waiters, who were at their stations on either side of the dining car, looked on curiously as the four children made their way along the aisle.

Pete stopped briefly before he reached the man in the checkered coat. Then, gathering his courage, he sprang forward and grabbed him by the arm.

"Don't try to get away, Mr. Barrow!" he commanded.

The man turned around, a look of surprise on his high-cheekboned face. Just as surprised as the Hollisters, he looked at them darkly. "You have made a mistake," he said icily.

Pete's face flushed. "We're very sorry, sir."

Seeing the commotion, the steward rushed up. Pete lamely told him of their search for a criminal. Then the stranger said, "We all make mistakes, but I'd advise you children to be more diplomatic in your search for the villain you want."

The steward started to chuckle, and now the Hollisters joined in the merriment over their funny mistake.

"We'll have to be very careful," Pete said. "If this should happen again, the conductor would probably put us off the train!"

The searchers became discouraged as they reached the next-to-the-last car in the long train without finding Mr. Barrow. Since the incident with the wrong man, they had seen nobody even faintly resembling him.

As the children stepped inside the coach, Pam said, "There's a blond fellow halfway up the car."

"I'll go first and take a look," Pete said.

As the other three lingered behind, he slowly walked along the aisle. If the fellow would only turn his head a bit so Pete could get a better look at him! But his face was buried in a newspaper.

Pete had to get virtually alongside the man before he could obtain a clear view of his face. As he did, the suspect looked up from his paper, saw Pete, and let out a cry of alarm.

"Mr. Barrow!" the boy shouted.

Without warning, Mr. Barrow jumped up, giving the boy a hard shove. Pete careened to the other side of the aisle, landing in the lap of a woman who was reading a magazine.

"Good gracious!" she cried, helping the boy to regain his balance.

Meanwhile Pam, Ricky, and Holly had dashed down the aisle after Mr. Barrow, who by now was opening the far door.

"Stop him! He's a thief!" Pam cried out.

As the children raced toward the rear of the car, they suddenly heard the noise of grinding brakes. The train was stopping! It halted with such abruptness that the Hollisters were thrown forward, sprawling along the aisle.

"Why did we stop?" Pam asked, pulling herself to her feet, half stunned by the shock.

"Mr. Barrow must have pulled the emergency cord," Pete said.

On their feet again, the children dashed toward the rear car. Entering it, they looked about. Mr. Barrow was nowhere in sight.

"There he goes!" Ricky shouted, pointing out the window. A man dashing into the bushes along the track was visible for only a moment, then he disappeared.

"Let's chase him!" Ricky urged.

"We can't," Pam said. "The train will start up again without us."

Just then the conductor opened the door. "What's going on here?" he cried. "Who pulled the emergency cord?"

The Hollisters quickly told their story. The conductor was amazed. "We can't stop to look for him now," he said, "but I'll report Mr. Barrow when we get to the next station." He gave the signal and the train started ahead again.

On their way back through the cars, the Hollisters were stopped by various people who asked whom they were chasing. When they reached the club car, Mrs. Hollister, who was wiping soda pop off her dress, asked why the train had stopped so suddenly. She was amazed to learn the reason, and that her children's deduction about Mr. Barrow had been correct.

"If he's going to Orient Harbor, we'll have to be on our guard," she said, adding that she would alert the police about the criminal as soon as they arrived.

In a little while the Hollisters went to the dining car for supper. The steward, upon hearing the children had spotted the phony movie man, was amazed.

Back in their rooms once more, the Hollisters found that the rhythmic *clickety-clack* of the rails made them sleepy and shortly all of them tumbled into their beds. But they were up at the first call for breakfast and hurried to the dining car.

"We're very close to Boston now," Mrs. Hollister said, glancing out the window just as they were finishing the meal.

Hurrying back to their compartments, the children eagerly watched the scenery unfold. Soon they were in the city proper and the train slowed down.

Mr. Barrow gave Pete a shove.

"North Station! North Station!" the porter called out, walking down the corridor and standing on the platform as the train slowed for the final stop.

"We're here!" Pete said excitedly as the porter lifted the steel plate covering the steps.

Pete was the first to hop to the platform, then he helped his mother and the others off the train.

"There's Tom King!" Ricky shouted gleefully as the Hawaiian hurried up to greet them.

"I knew we'd see you again!" Holly called, and Sue raced up and threw her arms around the young man.

"Aren't you happy to see us?" Holly asked, noticing a look of worry on the Hawaiian's face.

"I certainly am," he said, managing a smile, "but I'm afraid I have bad news about myself."

"What is it?" they all asked at once.

"Someone else is trying to claim my share of the fortune," he said.

CHAPTER 15

A TEA PARTY

THE reunion with Tom King, which was to have
been a happy one, had been saddened by his
announcement. The news that someone was
trying to claim his share of the family fortune
upset the children.

"How could anyone be so mean!" Holly
blurted.

"Who is this person?" Pete asked indignantly.

Tom said that the false claimant was unknown
to him, but the lawyer for the estate had said the
man possessed original drawings of the *Winged
Chief*.

"But they were stolen from you!" Pam declared.

"That's true, but how can I prove it?" Tom
said, shaking his head sadly.

"Don't worry," Pam begged Tom. "The ship's
log hasn't been found, and besides, don't forget
your grandmother's earring that will match your
tie clip."

"That's a long chance," the Hawaiian said.
"But you have given me courage. The Hollisters
don't give up easily, I see."

"And you shouldn't either," Pam said. "We're

going to look for clues for you while we're at Orient Harbor."

Tom told them that there would be a two-hour wait for the train which would take them to the seashore. Mrs. Hollister said this did not give time enough for any extensive sight-seeing in Boston, but they would ride around for an hour. Then they returned to the station, which had many little shops that interested the youngsters.

As they wandered about looking into the windows, Ricky tugged at Holly's arm and whispered, "I have a good idea." Taking his sister aside, he whispered in her ear.

"Oh goody," Holly said enthusiastically. "Just like in the ancient times."

Holly was in the habit of saying "ancient" about anything from her parents' childhood back to the beginning of the earth.

Ricky corrected her. "You mean colonial days," he said.

"No matter when it was," Holly giggled, "let's do it. And we'd better hurry."

"But first we'll have to buy some," Ricky said.

"Where will we get it?"

"I saw some stores across the street from the station," her brother answered. "Let's go there first."

Without being noticed by the rest of the family, Ricky and Holly walked through an arched doorway to the side of the station. Then they crossed the street and began to look in the shop windows for what they wanted.

"I don't see any grocery store," Holly said after they had walked a block.

"I think I see one down the street," Ricky told her. "Come on."

Holding his sister's hand, he led her down the busy street until they came to a small grocery.

"Do you have enough money?" Holly asked, looking questioningly at her brother.

For answer Ricky jingled some coins in his pocket. "Sure. And won't it be fun to do what the colonists did?"

"Oh yes," said Holly.

The children disappeared into the store but returned to the street in a few minutes. Ricky was carrying a small bag.

"We can't go there alone," Holly said as she glanced at a clock in a store window.

"We'll have time enough," Ricky said.

"Still I think Mother or Tom should take us."

"All right," Ricky said. "Let's go back to the station."

But after walking a block, they did not see North Station.

"It was here just a few minutes ago," Ricky said, scratching his head and looking around.

"It couldn't have moved," Holly told him.

"Then where did it go?" Ricky said, spinning

around on his heel and acting silly. "Maybe we walked two blocks, Holly. Follow me."

But after the children had walked two more blocks, they still had not found the station. All the time trucks and cars went driving past in the street, and the unfamiliar surroundings sent a small chill of anxiety through Holly.

Tugging nervously at one of her pigtails, she looked up at a street sign. "Commercial Street," she remarked.

"That should get us back to the station all right," Ricky said importantly.

"How do you know?"

"Well, there's commerce at the station, isn't there?" he asked.

This answer satisfied his sister for a while as they continued. Finally the little girl hesitated. "Ricky, I think we're lost."

"I—I do too," he agreed reluctantly. "I'll ask someone how to get back to the station."

But before he had a chance to speak to any of the passers-by, Holly cried out, "Look over there, Rick! The water front! Come on!"

The children hurried past a row of stores which sold ships' supplies until they came to a dock parallel with the street. They walked to the edge of it and looked down.

"Well, here's Boston Harbor." Ricky grinned. "Shall we do it now?"

"All right," Holly said, and her brother opened the bag he had been carrying.

He pulled out a small package of tea and ripped open the foil covering. Then he poured a handful into his sister's outstretched palm.

"Are you ready?" Ricky asked.

"Yes."

The children threw handfuls of the tea into Boston Harbor.

"Just like the people did long ago," Holly said.

Ricky put his hand to his mouth and made a noise like an Indian. "Now we can tell our friends we threw tea into Boston Harbor!" he said proudly.

As he glanced about, his eyes were attracted to a store window which displayed ships' lanterns and other equipment. Of particular interest was the figure of a wooden Indian mounted over the doorway.

"Let's get a better look," the boy said, pulling his sister by the hand. They crossed the street and looked up at the wooden Indian.

"I'll bet it's a figurehead," Holly said.

"Let's ask the man," Ricky suggested, and they walked into the store.

The clerk told them that the Indian figurehead had come from an old clipper ship. But when the children asked the name of it, the man said he did not know.

As they were about to leave the store, Holly

"I'll bet it's a figurehead."

glanced at a clock and cried out in fright, "Ricky, it's nearly time for our train!"

"We're going to have to run to make it."

"Maybe they'll leave without us," Holly said worriedly.

Hearing the children's conversation, the clerk called to them, "Where do you want to go?"

"North Station."

The man gave them directions and suggested that if they were in a hurry they had better take a cab. Ricky thanked him and they hurried out of the store.

"But we don't have money for a cab," Holly said, and tears began to trickle down her face.

"Then we'll have to run," her brother decided. "Let's see how fast we can go."

The two children raced along the sidewalk, weaving in and out among the pedestrians. They had gone no more than a block when they heard the sound of a siren.

"Fire engines!" Ricky cried out, glancing about.

"We can't stop to watch them," Holly said, tugging at his hand. "Come on, Ricky! Hurry!"

But as the siren grew louder, Ricky halted at the curb to watch. Up the street came a police car. It pulled to the curb alongside the children.

The driver, a handsome policeman, said in a broad Irish brogue, "Are you Ricky and Holly Hollister?"

"Why—yes," Holly replied, her mouth dropping open. "How did you know?"

"The whole Boston police force is looking for you," he said. "Come, climb in with me."

The children got into the car and the policeman set off again, his siren sounding. Then as he drove he picked up the microphone of his radio.

"Car 34 calling headquarters. I've found the Hollisters. Taking them to North Station."

A few minutes later, with brakes squealing, the policeman stopped the car in front of North Station and the children hopped out. They flew to their mother, who was standing on the curb waiting.

"We didn't mean to get lost!" Holly said, her eyes welling with tears.

"We threw tea into Boston Harbor just like in colonial days," Ricky said.

Mrs. Hollister was so overcome with relief at seeing her children again that she did not scold them. Instead she thanked the policeman, who saluted smartly and drove off. Then she and the two children hustled inside the station, where Tom King and the others waited.

"Hurry! Our train is due to pull out in one minute!" the Hawaiian said.

The whole group raced across the station and out onto the platform, where their baggage was piled neatly beside the train steps. After a porter had lifted the suitcases aboard, the Hollisters and Tom King trooped onto the train.

"Whew, I never thought we'd make it!" Tom said as he flopped into a seat and mopped his brow with a handkerchief.

"I think we found a clue to help you." Holly spoke up. "It's near the harbor."

She told about the Indian figurehead, adding, "Maybe it came from the *Winged Chief*."

Pete snapped his fingers. "Crickets! That's an idea. Do you suppose we can go back and inquire?"

"Not now, of course," Mrs. Hollister said. "I don't want to lose all of you."

Everybody laughed, and then settled back for the short trip to Orient Harbor. But Pam kept turning over in her mind the information about the Indian figurehead. She decided that if they by chance came to Boston during their vacation she would look it up and ask the store owner more questions about it.

The children were busy looking out at the marshy tidewater flats and little inlets as the train proceeded along the coast. Less than an hour later they pulled into a small town and the train stopped beside a quaint station. The name painted on it said ORIENT HARBOR.

"We're here! We're here!" Ricky shouted as he leaped up from his seat.

"I thought it was going to be a bigger place

than this," Pete said as he stepped down onto the platform.

Immediately a bearded man and a lovely woman greeted them. "Hello! It's so nice to see you again," Lisa Sarno said as Gregory Grant shook hands with the Hollisters and gave Sue a kiss.

After the baggage had been collected, Gregory said, "Right over this way. We have a limousine waiting for you."

A chauffeur piled the suitcases into the trunk of the limousine, and everyone got inside the long black vehicle. Pete and Ricky rode up front with the chauffeur.

Pam and Holly occupied two little folding seats while the adults sat in back, Greg holding Sue on his lap.

"We have a surprise for you," Lisa said as they drove along.

When the children asked eagerly what it was, she told them the script had been changed slightly so as to include the Hollisters.

"And guess what you youngsters are going to be in the movie?" Greg said.

"Pirates?" Ricky asked.

"Of course not," Lisa said, chuckling. "You are going to be the captain's children in a very important scene!"

CHAPTER 16

HALF A SHIP

HAPPY exclamations arose from the children, and Pam said, "If we're to be the captain's children, who is going to play the captain?"

"Greg is," Lisa replied.

Sue rolled her eyes and giggled. "My movie daddy!" she said, and hugged the actor.

But despite all the gaiety, Tom King seemed very sober. Pam felt certain that something else was bothering him besides the trouble over his inheritance, but she decided not to ask him about it until later.

In a few minutes the limousine pulled up in front of a small hotel. "All the movie people are staying here," Lisa said as they piled out.

"It's not the finest hotel in the world," Greg said with a wink, "but it's quaint and comfortable."

After Mrs. Hollister had signed the register, a small, elderly bellman, wearing a faded blue uniform but no cap, directed them to a tiny elevator. It was so narrow that it could hold only two persons at one time.

After showing the visitors how to operate it, he stepped back and Mrs. Hollister and Pam got on. Pam pressed the button for the third floor. When the car stopped, she opened the tiny door and they stepped into a bare corridor. The Hollisters' suite consisted of three small rooms and a bath.

Pam chuckled when she looked at the tub. It stood on four legs and was very short.

"This must have been built for a midget," the girl said, laughing.

The other children soon followed, and the Hollisters made themselves at home in their new quarters. Pam excused herself, however, and went downstairs to talk with Tom King.

"Why are you so downhearted?" she asked kindly as they seated themselves on a sofa in the lobby.

"I've run out of money to continue my search," Tom said, his eyes staring at the floor. "Bad luck has trailed me every step of the way."

"If it's the sketches you're worried about," Pam declared, "I'm sure the photostat studio in Shoreham will testify that you had the originals."

Then she promised again that the Hollisters would look for the logbook of the old *Winged Chief* clipper ship, and also try to find the matching earring that had belonged to Tom's grandmother.

The young man put his hand over Pam's and said, "You Hollisters are wonderfully kind, but

I have made up my mind. I'm leaving for Hawaii tomorrow night."

"Oh, but you can't!" Pam protested. "You may be very close to solving your mystery without even knowing it."

Tom grinned and declared that he would try to be cheerful for the rest of his stay at Orient Harbor. "Maybe we can have some fun tomorrow," he said. Then he said good-by and went to a little rooming house down the street where he was staying.

After breakfast in the hotel dining room next morning, Greg and Lisa met the Hollisters in the lobby and introduced them to the movie director, Mr. Powell. He was about their father's age, with broad shoulders, wavy hair, and a pleasant smile.

"Glad to meet all the Happy Hollisters," he said.

The director explained that they had built a big set for the movie at Newman's Wharf. "It really looks like a clipper ship," he said.

Mr. Powell ushered the group to the company limousine, which took them to the wharf. It was located on a neck of land which jutted out into the harbor. At the end of it was a clipper ship.

"How wonderful!" Nan exclaimed.

Holly was gleeful. "A real ship! Does it sail?"

The man grinned. "No," he confessed. "It's only a set." The director explained that the side of the ship facing them and the deck looked like a real clipper ship. "But it's only half a ship," he said. "There is no other side to it."

"Then how will you get pictures of the clipper ship sailing on the ocean?" Ricky asked.

"We do that with a toy model," Mr. Powell replied. "It will look so real that no one will notice the difference."

The Hollisters got out of the car and walked toward the end of the wharf, where workmen were busy putting final touches on the clipper ship set.

"You children will be in two scenes," Mr. Powell told them. "And I'd like you to practice your parts today, if you will." He called to an assistant to bring the children's scripts. "Read them carefully," Mr. Powell requested.

With Mrs. Hollister helping the younger children, they eagerly studied the lines. Then the director explained that the first scene would portray the maiden trip of the *Winged Chief*. In it Pam and Sue would serve tea to their father, the captain, on the deck of the clipper.

"The rest of you will be having fun," he said, "because the maiden trip is always one of gaiety."

"It says here I'm to climb the rigging." Pete spoke up, grinning broadly.

"And I'm to peek out of the lifeboat," Ricky chortled.

The script stated that Holly was to sit on a small cannon as if riding a horse.

"We'll practice the scene without costumes," Mr. Powell said.

Another one of his assistants marked spots on the deck where the actors were to stand. With Greg taking his place as the ship's captain, the children went through their routine without saying their lines.

Holly found the little brass cannon and straddled it, waving her hand as if she were atop a bucking bronco. Pete climbed the rigging and peered out over the harbor, while Ricky shinned up into the lifeboat and peeked out impishly.

Pam now took a silver tray holding a teapot, sugar bowl and creamer, and a small china cup. Coming up out of the companionway with Sue following, she approached Captain Greg.

"Curtsy!" the director called out. And both girls did this gracefully.

"That's fine!" Mr. Powell said. "Your lines are very simple. As Pam offers the tea to the captain, she will say, 'It's teatime, Father.' Then Sue will say, 'It came from China by clipper.' "

"All right, let's try it again," Mr. Powell said.

As the girls came onto the deck, Tom King arrived on the set and unconsciously they glanced in his direction.

"Keep your mind on your acting!" the director called. "Look at the captain!"

The sudden command rattled Pam and Sue.

"Curtsy!" the director called out.

Instead of walking slowly, they hurried toward Gregory Grant.

"It's teatime, Father," Pam said as both girls curtsied.

"It came all the way by China from clipper," Sue lisped. Then, realizing her mistake, she started to giggle.

Pam turned toward her sister and whispered, "Don't do that, Sue!" She herself was so excited that she let the tea tray tilt. The pot skidded forward and Greg grabbed it just in time.

"Hold it!" the director called.

Sue burst into tears. "I—I spoiled everything!" she said as her mother hurried over to console her.

"It happens to the best of us," Mr. Powell said, trying to soothe the little girl. "Come now, we'll do it over again." And this time the scene was perfect.

"In a little while we'll try it in costume and before the cameras," the director said, adding, "The sets are not entirely ready for the rescue scene, so how would you children like a ride in the lifeboat?"

"That would be great!" Ricky said, climbing back on deck.

Pete came down from the rigging. "Will we use this lifeboat, Mr. Powell?" he asked.

The director said no, that was only a prop. "There's another lifeboat alongside the wharf. It has a small outboard motor concealed in it so we won't have to row."

Mrs. Hollister said she would remain behind to chat with Lisa and look over another one of the sets which showed the interior of the captain's cabin. "It's not really authentic," Lisa told her. "In the cabin of the real *Winged Chief* there was a picture painted on the wall showing a clipper ship race. No one has been able to find the original, so we can't make a true copy of it."

As she continued to talk with Mrs. Hollister, the children, Tom King, Greg, and Mr. Powell walked back along the wharf to where the lifeboat, called the *Swan*, was moored.

"I'll manage the motor for you," Tom King said. "At home I have one just like it."

"It's all yours, skipper," Mr. Powell said as the little group stepped into the lifeboat.

The director explained that he would like to show the children the other side of the half ship, on which the carpenters still were working. Pete cast off and Tom King started the motor. With a *put-put-put*, the lifeboat pulled away from the dock.

"You can skirt around the other side of the set," Mr. Powell said, and Tom did this.

"There really isn't any boat at all over here!" Holly said, amazed.

They cruised around while Greg and Mr. Powell explained to the children how movie sets were built. Often scenes were painted back to back on one big frame, he told them. Then he changed the subject. "How would you all like a little ride around the harbor?"

"That would be keen!" Pete said.

The harbor was about a half mile wide, with a rocky shore on either side.

"Let's ride out to that buoy and back again, Tom," Mr. Powell said, pointing to a bell-shaped object bobbing in the water near the mouth of the harbor.

The lifeboat was not so speedy as some of the craft the Hollisters had seen on Pine Lake. But what fun it was to ride out in the harbor! The sun shone down through fleecy clouds and sea gulls wheeled about in the sky. Several motorboats and a sailboat passed close by, and the children waved to the occupants.

Presently they came to the buoy, which rocked back and forth in the water. Tom rounded it and headed back toward the wharf. Just then a speedboat came in from the ocean toward them.

"Wow, look at him go!" Ricky cried.

"He shouldn't be going that fast in the harbor," Mr. Powell said. "It isn't safe with other boats around."

The oncoming craft did not slacken speed. "He's heading toward us!" Pete shouted.

Everyone in the *Swan* held his breath for a moment, hoping that the speedboat would veer off to one side. But instead it bore down on them.

"He's going to crash into us!" Pam cried in terror. The other children were so frightened that they could not utter a sound.

Tom King tried to maneuver his craft out of the way. He nearly succeeded, but the speedboat, its driver hunched over the wheel, crashed into the stern of the *Swan*.

Everyone was jolted and the lifeboat tilted over at a dangerous angle.

The Hollister children screamed as Tom, Greg, and Mr. Powell tried to right the craft.

But it was too late. As the speedboat streaked away toward the sea again, the *Swan* flipped over, throwing everybody into the water!

CHAPTER 17

AN AMAZING DISCOVERY

PETE was the first to bob to the surface of the water. He saw Ricky and Holly, stunned by the collision, doing their best to swim but floundering helplessly.

"Get Holly!" Pete called to Pam, who came through the waves to his side. He himself swam toward Ricky. Tom King, meanwhile, had surfaced and was looking about. He spied little Sue, some distance away, sputtering and flailing her arms.

With magnificent long strokes, Tom quickly reached Sue. Grabbing her, he told her to ride on his back as he swam toward the *Swan*.

He reached it at the same time as Pete and Pam, who had Ricky and Holly in tow. Greg, in the meantime, was swimming around in circles and diving. Waving his arms, he shouted, "Powell has disappeared!"

Instantly Tom dived deep. Seconds passed as the children watched anxiously and righted the lifeboat. Where could Mr. Powell be?

When the Hawaiian did not reappear himself, the children's worry was doubled. "He's been out of sight a minute," Pete said. "How can he stay under that long?"

Just then Tom bobbed to the surface, gripping a limp Mr. Powell, and began to tow him to the boat. With Greg's and Pete's aid, Mr. Powell was rolled into the lifeboat. Tom crawled aboard and quickly began artificial respiration on the unconscious man. Presently Mr. Powell's eyes fluttered open and he gasped, "Where—where am I?"

"You're safe," Pam said. "Tom rescued you."

Once the director was out of danger, everyone praised the Hawaiian for his heroic efforts.

"It was nothing," he said bashfully. "In Hawaii I practically live in the water." He tried the motor, but the crash had disabled it.

"We'll have to row to shore," Tom said finally, lifting two oars from the bottom of the boat.

He manned one of them while Pete and Ricky took the other. Greg and the others made Mr. Powell comfortable in the bottom of the boat.

Tom asked if anyone had noticed who the driver of the speedboat was. Because the fellow had been bending low, no one had been able to get a good look at him.

"Why would he hit us on purpose?" Pam asked.

Tom surmised that the man was trying to injure only him so he could not collect the inheritance.

Holly said she had a good look at the speedboat itself, however. "It was white and had two little red anchors painted on the bow," she said.

"Good girl!" Tom said. "That will identify it."

When they reached the dock, Mrs. Hollister and a group of movie people met them. They had not seen the accident and were shocked to hear of it.

After the children had hopped ashore, Greg and Tom helped Mr. Powell, who was feeling much better. "I'll never be able to thank you enough for saving my life," he said.

The director explained that he had been knocked partly unconscious by the collision, and had finally ceased struggling. He would have drowned had it not been for the Hawaiian.

He smiled at Tom and added, "Would you consider working with us in the movie we're making? We have a rescue scene which needs a good swimmer. You're just the man for it."

Tom said he would be delighted to take the job.

"Then you're signed up now," Mr. Powell concluded.

The Hawaiian grinned broadly and said that since he now had a job he would be able to stay at Orient Harbor. The children were thrilled.

Mr. Powell called the cast together and said that rehearsals would stop for several days until he felt stronger.

Pam whispered to her brother, "This will give us time to do some more sleuthing."

"Let's go to the museum tomorrow," Pete suggested.

Next morning, while Mrs. Hollister took the other children on a sight-seeing tour, Pete and Pam hurried to the museum. Going straight to Mr. Dooley, they introduced themselves. He seemed glad to meet them.

When they asked if he had any books telling about the remaining days of the clipper ships, he replied, "We have a few. Come this way."

He led them into a small library and pulled a book from a shelf. It was titled *Last Days of the Clippers*.

How interesting it was! From the book the children learned that clippers were used for many years and as late as 1900 one of them plied between Italy and South America. But the fate of the others had not been so kind. Several were wrecked on Cape Horn. Others had burned. Unfortunately there was no record of what had happened to the *Winged Chief*.

"The movie folks told me they couldn't find out about that one either," Mr. Dooley said. "Say, how would you like to look at the exhibits?"

"We'd love to," Pam replied.

The old man led them from one room to another, showing exhibits of olden days and models of old clipper ships. Next he led them into the Polynesian Room, saying he must leave them.

"Oh, what a wonderful place!" Pam exclaimed.

The room was full of trinkets and curios which clipper ship captains had brought back from the Pacific Islands. Pam admired the grass skirts and intricately carved jewelry while Pete was taken with the shark-tooth swords and shields used by natives.

"Look at this, Pete!" Pam said presently, walking over to a grotesquely carved face on a pedestal.

Pete read the inscription near the base. It was an idol which had been worshiped by the natives. Then in smaller print it said, *a gift from the captain of the* Winged Chief.

"Crickets!" Pete exclaimed. "This may be a good clue!"

There was no further information on the idol, so Pam said, "Let's look on the underside."

"All right," Pete said. "I'll tilt it a bit and you look."

As Pete did this, Pam gasped. A small piece of paper, brown with age, had been pasted on the base. On it was scribbled in old-fashioned script: *THE WINGED CHIEF ORIENT HARBOR* 1849 *BOSTON* 1890.

Pete quickly set the face back on its pedestal.

"That means the ship ended her days somewhere in Boston Harbor," the boy surmised.

The children hurried to tell Mr. Dooley about their find. "Hmm," the curator said. "Many clipper ships were dismantled in Boston."

"This may lead us to the logbook of the *Winged Chief!*" Pam said excitedly.

Mr. Dooley agreed, but added that the chances of finding it after so many years were one in a thousand.

The children hurried back to the hotel. Their family had returned from their sight-seeing tour.

"We want to go to Boston right away!" Pam said, and told the reason.

"I think we should start our search at the figurehead Ricky and Holly discovered," Pete added.

Mrs. Hollister said she had promised Lisa to attend a meeting of the historical society that afternoon. "But perhaps Tom will take you," she said.

Pam called him on the telephone, and he said he would be delighted to take them on the train after lunch.

By three o'clock they were at the North Station, and hurried along the street to the place where the figurehead looked down from the water-front building.

"I've never played detective before," Tom said, grinning, as they walked into the store.

This time Pete asked the clerk whether the figurehead had come from the *Winged Chief*.

"I think it did," the man replied.

"Do you know who put it on this building?"

The clerk said he did not know, but referred the children to the building's owner, who lived nearby. With Sue tugging at Tom's hand, the children raced to the man's house and rang the doorbell. A middle-aged man answered it.

When Pete asked about the figurehead, he said, "You'll have to see my uncle about that. He was in charge of dismantling the *Winged Chief*."

"Yikes!" Ricky exclaimed. "He must be awful old!"

The man agreed. "Uncle Joe is one of the oldest men in Boston. But his memory is good and I know he will be glad to answer your questions."

He gave them the address of a small house about a quarter of a mile away and bade the Hollisters good-by.

Uncle Joe himself answered the Hollisters' knock. "Oh, young visitors!" he said. "Glad to see you!"

When Pete asked about the *Winged Chief*, the old man said, "Come in and sit down. I'll tell you what I know."

He ushered them into his quaint little apartment. It reminded the children very much of Mr. Sparr's place at Shoreham. There was a ship model on a table and a big helm over his gas-burning fireplace.

When Pam told him they were searching for the log of the *Winged Chief*, the old fellow rubbed a bony hand against his half-bald head. "Many people have tried to find that," he said, "but no one has. The whereabouts of that old logbook is one of the mysteries of Boston Harbor."

"What happened to the ship?" Ricky asked.

Uncle Joe said it had been dismantled under his guidance and the timbers used to build a fish market.

"Near here?" Pete asked.

"Down the water front a bit," the old man said, and added, "Customers liked that old picture too."

"You mean the one from the captain's cabin?" Pam asked.

"That's right," Uncle Joe answered. "It was put behind the counter in the fish store and was there for years."

"We're looking for that too!" Pam cried.

"Could you take us to the old market?" Pete asked Uncle Joe.

The old man said he could not move out of his apartment because of his arthritis, but he gave the Hollisters and Tom King the directions.

"Thank you," Pete said as they left. "We'll go there right away."

Tom had trouble keeping up with the children as they half walked, half ran toward the old fish market. A block from the location on the water front they heard loud banging and hammering.

"It sounds as if someone's tearing down a building," Pete remarked.

A frightened look came into Pam's eyes. "You don't suppose——"

"I'm afraid it is!" said Tom.

Big dump trucks were standing in front of a partly razed building. Alongside it was a crane with a ball swinging at the end of a cable. It kept crashing against the side of the building. As the debris fell to the sidewalk, a power shovel picked up beams and plaster and loaded them onto one of the trucks.

"Oh dear," Pam said as she surveyed the scene, brokenhearted. "Now we'll never find the logbook!"

"Don't be too sure of that," Pete said as he went up to one of the workmen. "Is this the place where the old fish market was?" he asked.

"Yes, the fish market did occupy part of this building," the workman answered. "But we hauled that section away yesterday."

Pete asked where the debris was, and the man told him it had been carried to a vacant lot on the next street.

"Just around the corner from here," he said.

The youngsters outdistanced Tom King in

Pam brushed away plaster dust.

their race to the vacant lot. The old beams, boards, broken plaster, and doorframes lay in a tangled jumble.

The children swarmed over the debris looking carefully for anything which might prove to be a clue. Finally Pam spied a long, rectangular piece of wood thick with plaster dust. Running her hand over the surface of it, she exclaimed:

"It's the old mural!"

Pete helped her brush away more of the dust. Beneath was revealed a beautiful though faded picture of a clipper ship race.

Hastily the children began to wipe away more of the white film. Suddenly Holly's hands brushed over a raised portion of the wood.

CLICK! A small panel slid back, revealing a tiny cubbyhole. Inside it was a black book!

CHAPTER 18

A PUZZLE SOLVED

WITH a gasp, Pam reached for the old book and quickly opened it.

"The log of the *Winged Chief!*" Pete shouted.

"This is marvelous!" Tom King said, as excited as the youngsters.

"Can we take it back to Orient Harbor?" Ricky asked.

The Hawaiian said the mural and the book did not rightly belong to them. "I'll go see the foreman of the wrecking crew," he said, "and try to buy these things. Wait here for me." Then he disappeared around the corner.

"Please see what the log says about the ancient wedding," Ricky begged.

"All right," Pam replied, her eyes glistening. She was about to open the book when suddenly a man climbed over the debris toward them. He was roughly dressed and had long, unkempt hair under a peaked cap.

"What are you doing?" he shouted.

"Looking for something," Pete said.

"You've no business here," the man said gruffly.

"Who are you?" Pam asked.

The fellow said he was a watchman and had been ordered not to let anyone take things from the lot.

"What did you find?" he called out, approaching Pam.

"An old book, and we're going to buy it."

"Give it to me!" the fellow said as he snatched the book from Pam's hands. He tugged the peaked cap down lower over his eyes and made off in the opposite direction. But in his haste he tripped on a protruding board and stumbled forward. As he tried to regain his balance, off came his cap, and a wig with it.

"It's Barrow!" Pete shouted.

"Tom, Tom, come here quick!" Pam cried out as the Hawaiian appeared around the corner.

"What happened?"

"Barrow stole the logbook!" Pam cried.

"We'll catch him!" Tom and Pete led the chase after Barrow. The fellow ran to a dock and jumped into a speedboat. Pete saw that it had two little red anchors on the bow.

"He's the one who ran into us!" the boy shouted.

Barrow pressed the starter button. The motor sputtered to life and the boat started off.

"Come back, come back!" Pam shouted.

"We'll get him somehow," Tom King said, his jaw set grimly.

As Pete looked around for another boat, they

suddenly noticed that Barrow's motor had stopped. The fugitive tinkered with it furiously.

"No doubt the collision damaged it," Pete said. "Oh, I wish we could find another boat to chase him with!"

Suddenly Tom stripped off his shirt. "I'm going in!"

"Me, too," Pete said, kicking off his shoes.

With neat dives they plunged into the harbor and started swimming toward the disabled boat.

Barrow desperately tried to repair the motor as Tom and Pete drew near him. On shore the Hollisters shouted encouragement. "Catch him, Tom! Get him, Pete!"

The Hawaiian was first to reach the boat. As he put his hand on the gunwale, the motor came to life again.

"Get away from here!" Barrow shouted as Pete grabbed the other side of the boat.

Barrow gunned the motor and the speedboat knifed through the water, dragging the two swimmers alongside of it.

As Tom hoisted himself up to the gunwale, Barrow gave him a shove. The Hawaiian fell backward but still kept his grip on the craft.

Pete, meanwhile, started wriggling in from the other side. Then, as Barrow turned his attention to the boy, Tom scrambled over the side.

Barrow wheeled and picked up a wrench. But as he raised it to hit Tom, Pete rolled into the boat and banged into the criminal's legs, throwing him off balance. The wrench never landed. Tom grasped the man by the wrist and twisted it until the weapon fell to the bottom of the boat.

"You'll never get that book!" Barrow hissed as he struggled to free himself. With his left hand he reached under a tarpaulin and drew out the log. "I'll throw it over——" he cried.

But Pete was too quick for him. He grabbed the book and wrenched it free. Now the criminal lay on the bottom of the boat, his arms pinned at his sides.

"Tie him up, Pete," Tom ordered as Barrow cried out defiantly.

Pete reached for the mooring rope and in a few minutes had the sullen fellow tied securely. Then, with Tom at the wheel, the speedboat headed back to the harbor.

By the time they landed at the dock, Pam had summoned a policeman. Tom lifted Barrow to his feet and shoved him into the officer's arms.

"The Hollister children have told me about you," he said. "Come with me." The policeman led the captive to a waiting prowl car.

"You Hollisters!" the fellow snarled. "My pals and I could have had——" Realizing he was saying too much, Barrow shut up like a clam.

"He'll talk more before we're through with him," the policeman said. "I'll see you at the station house later," he told Tom. "You can make

Barrow wheeled and picked up a wrench.

a detailed report of the charges against this man."

After the police car had driven away, the Hollisters and Tom King sat down on the dock to read the old logbook. Presently Pam came to the page which told of the wedding on shipboard.

"Here it is, Tom!" she cried. "And look at this!"

On the opposite page was a rare tintype of the bridal couple.

"You look very much like your grandmother," Pete remarked. "If this doesn't clinch your case with the inheritance lawyers, nothing will!"

Pam turned the page and again her eyes glowed with excitement. Another entry stated that the captain would give the earring to his favorite niece, Nancy Bowers.

"You'll be lucky if she's still alive," Pam said with a sigh.

"Let's try to look her up right away," Holly suggested.

First Tom and the children carried the old mural from the trash heap and hailed a taxicab. The driver obligingly tied it to the top of his car and drove them all back to the station. By this time Pete's and Tom's clothes had been fairly well dried out by the sun and wind, so after Tom checked the mural with the baggage master, Pete scanned the Boston telephone book for Nancy Bowers.

"Perhaps she married and has a different

name," Pam said worriedly as Pete found a listing.

"Well, it's worth a try," Pete said, going into the booth.

After making a call, the boy stepped out of the phone booth, his face wreathed with smiles.

"She *was* the right one!" he said. "She's old and lives in the Back Bay section."

"Come on, we'll see her right away," Pam said.

It did not take long for them to reach the address.

"Come in," a sweet elderly woman invited them. "I understand you found my uncle's logbook."

Pete read her the entry about the earring and the old lady said, "Yes, I'll never forget the time he gave it to me, and I still have it. Would you like to see it?"

She went into her bedroom, opened a jewel box, and returned with the earring. In every way it matched the one on Tom King's tie clasp.

"We'd like to borrow this for evidence." Tom spoke up.

"Of course, you may," the old lady said.

Tom smiled at her kindly. "In return, perhaps you would like to read your uncle's diary."

Nancy Bowers said she would be happy to do this when Tom King had finished using it.

Jubilantly Tom and the Hollisters hurried back

to Orient Harbor. Tom telephoned the lawyers handling the inheritance case. When they heard his evidence they agreed there was no doubt that he would receive the money.

"But what about the other claimant?" Tom asked.

"I understand the fellow got in trouble and is in jail," the Hawaiian was told.

"Is his name Barrow?"

"That's right."

After Tom King hung up he returned to the Hollisters. "Barrow was trying to get the fortune for himself."

"I hope they catch the fellows who were helping him," Pete said.

This turned out to be the case. For next day, when Tom appeared in Boston to prefer charges against Barrow, he was told that the prisoner had confessed, implicating two henchmen. Upon his return to Orient Harbor, the Hawaiian had the full story. He went immediately to the Hollisters' hotel to relate what Barrow had confessed.

The criminal had followed Tom, looking for an opportunity to steal the sketches of the clipper ship.

"Was he the one who followed us the night we went for ice cream?" Pam asked.

"Right. He admitted that."

Barrow also had instructed his henchmen to rob Tom on his way to Orient Harbor.

182

"Why did he ride up on the train with us?" Pam asked.

"That was only by accident," Tom informed them. "And a bad one for him!"

"But why would he try to injure all of you in the harbor with his speedboat?" Mrs. Hollister wondered.

"As Pam guessed," Tom said, "he wanted to get me out of the way so I could not claim the inheritance."

Meanwhile the movie people were happy to get the original mural which had hung in the captain's cabin on the *Winged Chief*. Artists had quickly gone to work on it and now the touched-up picture looked as good as new.

"We'll use it in the cabin set," the director told the youngsters next day.

Then he added, "I have a surprise for all of you." He led them to a small dressing room under the deck of the make-believe clipper. "Here are your costumes," he said.

The children squealed with delight when they saw what they were to wear. The girls had frilly dresses with pantaloons and cute little bonnets, while the boys were provided with sailor suits.

"Now we'll do the scene live," Mr. Powell said. "Do you remember your lines?"

Laughing, the children said that they did.

Ricky shinned into the lifeboat, Pete climbed up into the rigging, Holly sat on the little brass cannon, and Pam and Sue disappeared down the companionway.

"Roll 'em!" Mr. Powell cried. Everything aboard the set became hushed as the two girls came into the scene with the tray of tea. They approached the captain with graceful steps, spoke their lines, and curtsied.

"Beautifully done!" the director called out when the scene was over. "Hurray for the Happy Hollisters!"